Fuerte:

A Journey Continued

Written by

Marcelino Rosas

Printed in the United States of America

First Printing, 2014

ISBN 978-0-9859437-1-4

Proud Peacock Publishing LLC

ProudPeacockPublishing@ymail.com

Dedicated to my wonderful husband Pieter.

This book is for you.

Foreword

In *Afuera*, Roberto Salas came of age by discovering his sexuality, dealing with his family, finding first love and forming deep friendships. Now on his own in a new city, Roberto hopes for a fresh start. But new beginnings bring new challenges; work, school, and sex compete for his time. How will he juggle them all when life throws him some unexpected curve balls? "Fuerte: A Journey Continued", delves into Roberto's discovery that being a young adult in Los Angeles, away from everything he knows, is far crazier than anything his past has prepared him for.

Special thanks to Nicholas J. Gallardi, Phillip J. Bartell, and John Pachl. I could not have done it with out all your love and support. You contributed more to this book than you really know. I'll be forever thankful.

Cover photo by Kurt R. Brown.
Cover design made by Camrin William.
Book edited by Jesse James Manning and John Pachl.

Fuerte: A Journey continued, is a work of literary fiction that I wrote over many years and countless drafts. I conceived this as a contemporary rendering of the traditional roman à clef, popular in the nineteenth century, which incorporates portraits of the author's contemporaries and his own experiences overlaid with fiction. No real names are used. Some characters are composite creations, while others are entirely imaginary. Every character, regardless of whether they are inspired by real persons or events, has been crafted by my own language and style to become a part of my book's narrative. This is in no way a biography, memoir or historical account of my life or anyone else's life.

This is a disclaimer: if you are too young, or easily offended by gay sex or the discussion of it, you should probably stop reading now. Or if this is Mom, definitely stop reading now.

Contents

Fuerte: A Journey continued

PROLOGUE

Someone wryly observed that, if we all knew what life had in store for us over the course of our lifetime, we'd be afraid to get out of bed. More optimistic people counter that, if we knew the future, there'd be no point in living; it would all be mapped out for us and we'd just be going through the motions of living.

As a work of fiction, some of these events are based on my life. Some are not. What I have omitted are the occasional times of disillusion, prolonged sadness, loneliness. Why dwell on these things? Unless we are terribly unlucky, these are bumps in the road, not the road itself.

So while this story may at times seem to be about a guy who had it easier than you, remember this: so many times I had to repeat to myself over and over that, despite all the setbacks and the sadness and the uncertainty, at least I was standing on my own two feet.

The problem was, being a realist, I often had to admit to myself that even though I was standing on my own two feet, it felt like I was standing in quicksand.

That's life: one tradeoff after another. But we push on; we persevere. There are times when we think life isn't worth it anymore, but then a new chapter in our life begins; one of the reasons I divided this book into chapters.

You see, nothing stayed the same very long. If your life seems stagnant, maybe you need a big change: a move to another city; a different relationship; testing the possibility of religious faith... whatever works for you.

Cher once observed that, "Life is not a dress rehearsal." We only have one chance at this life. If you are unhappy, find a way to change your situation. Sometimes that change can be small; it might have to be drastic. But in the end, your life will change, and if you planned it well, odds are it will be for the better.

Introduction

Welcome back to my INNER mind.

Writers sometimes admit they get choked up while writing; it's natural and often inevitable. The writing process can bring back all sorts of memories and emotions; some we don't even understand ourselves.

But this time what packed the biggest emotional punch was not something I wrote, but a letter received from a young man in Hawaii who wrote how his sexuality made him feel alienated and alone. He was debating suicide. But reading my first book, Afuera, helped him believe that life will eventually get better, and maybe love is around the corner. So readers: believe and persevere!

In this second book, Fuerte, I've written about the struggles of being on your own two feet. Everyone dreams of not living with the restrictions of one's parents, but then reality sets in.

I've seen many young, hopeful people come into Los Angeles from their small hometowns. It's sad, but most end up homeless. They are forced to go back home with their tail between their legs, having failed to make it in Hollywood, and ripe for their parents to say, "See? I told you so!"

We have to accept that life is hard when you are an adult. Things get real very fast and hard when suddenly you have to pay rent and work just to eat. But with a lot of hard work, some luck, and a good support system, anything is possible. Be strong, everyone. Be fuerte.

Chapter One:

New Adventure

I'm 30,000 feet in the air, in the last seat on the left side of the airplane by the window; I'm waiting impatiently for it to land. The flight was only two-and-a-half hours long, but it felt a lot longer. I just couldn't wait to get to our destination: my soon-to-be new home in Los Angeles, California.

My mind wandered to something my mother once told me: "God only gives us what we can handle." I hope she was right. The pilot's voice snaps me out of my inner thoughts and says, "We will be landing in about 20 minutes in the great city of Los Angeles. Please fasten your seat belts, and thanks again for flying with us."

Nerves started to kick in, followed by fear, and ending with excitement. After leaving the beautiful state of Washington and being heartbroken by my first gay love, Hunter, here I was, 20 years old and trying to make a new life for myself; a fresh start, even if I didn't have much of a plan or direction as to what exactly I'd be doing.

Since Sheldon (my best friend who was now a cancer survivor) refused to let me pay for rent while I stayed with him; I had saved up quiet a bit of money in the years I spent working in the Northwest. I had about $20,000 in my bank account, plus a credit card that I would use in cases of emergency. My plan was simple: First, find a cheap hotel or hostel to stay somewhere in the Los Angeles area ... preferably in West Hollywood; secondly, find a job (or two); and third, finish my studies. I left before graduating at the University of Washington. I finished my Associates degree a couple years prior, and I was so close to finishing my English degree. Maybe UCLA or USC would have a place for me. Once I was settled in, I needed to find a regular apartment. I was open to having a roommate, since it was so expensive to live in the city.

That was it, my amazing plan. It wasn't much, but it was something, and other than that ... everything else was a complete blank.

I was happy and carefree before my flight to Los Angeles. Then my mother called. Instant nerves. Instant tension. Honestly, I was more nervous than I had been in years. The conversation went something like this:

"How's my little munchkin?" the sweet voice on the other end of the phone asked.

"Good, good," I said, almost subconsciously.

" Oh yeah?"

"Yeah ... why?"

"Just asking."

"Ooookay." Now I was starting to wonder where the questioning was leading.

"What are you up to?"

Darn it! When will I learn my mom knows everything? She's like the mythical Greek Hydra, but with eyes and ears everywhere.

"Ha! You know don't you?" I exclaimed.

"Yes, I hear you are moving back to California."

"Sheldon doesn't need me in the house anymore. Just looking for my own place."

"Really?"

"Yeah, no biggie."

"I know what type of place you'd like: plenty of windows, nice southernly view, close to a gym, familiar zip code..."

The phone almost dropped out of my hands.

"I'm waiting to board the flight to L.A. now. How did you find out?"

"Sheldon told me."

Mental note to self: stop acting like such a Boy Scout and cover your tracks. Idiot!

"Of course he did."

"Well, come stay with us. You can live in the small apartment behind our new house. It has its own driveway and everything."

I knew this would be coming...

"That's sweet of you to offer, but I think I'll be good on my own," I stammered back.

"Why? Don't you want to be close to your mother?"

"I do, and I'll visit constantly, but I'm a grown up now. I have to go out in the world and make something of myself; someone you'd be proud of. I need to make my own path." I hoped she'd understand.

"I'm already proud of you," she said sweetly.

"You know what I mean..."

"Of course. If you need anything just give me or your dad a call."

"Okay. Thank you! I have to go … people are starting to board the plane."

At this point, simultaneous thoughts raced through my mind: feelings of guilt and remorse; that I keep so many things secret; go months at a time without even calling my parents, wanting to keep my move a secret from everyone, and now wondering why. My mother gives me unconditional support. Why do I hide things from her? All this fear, self-loathing and guilt is a cocktail of disasters for the positive, carefree mood I had just minutes ago. Whatever you say next mom, I thought, don't say, "I love you."

"Love you," comes my mother's gentle voice over the phone.

This is going to be a long flight.

On the positive side, at least it gave me time to think. Sure it would be easy to just move back to my parent's new house out in Palm Springs, but what good would that do me? I know my parents are slowly coming around to the idea that I'm gay. My mom fully understands me now, but my father, on the other hand, has it in his mind that, "Sure, he might be 'gay,' but he can still change if he wants to."

He believes that I just have to be secluded from other gay people who do nothing but tempt me. Once sheltered from the world, I would eventually come around and grow an attraction to women. That's how he thought things worked. I knew that if I were to move in with them, I'd be giving him false hope and power over me again. He's a bit ignorant like that, but at least he has come to terms about me being gay. Having him talk to me again and loving me in his own way was better than nothing. What else could I ask for? Maybe in time I'd get a chance to really educate him about the gay world. What I told my mother wasn't a lie. I needed to create my own path. Sure, I had grown plenty already in Washington, but it was now time to stand on my own two feet.

As the plane descended toward the runway, my mind wandered once again to my bittersweet time in Washington. Thoughts rushed through my head like an old movie reel playing over and over. I saw Hunter (the closeted gay Mormon) when we went on our first date. I saw our first kiss. In my mind I relived us laying in bed together in perfect bliss. Then I replayed my heartbreak when he broke off our relationship with a cold, heartless text message: "I'm sorry I can't do it."

I saw the faces of my friends Amber and Rose when I first met them and when I left them. I saw Sheldon and all his stages of cancer: the shaving of his hair, the running to the bathroom to throw up, the crying sessions at night trying to cheer him up, to him finally beating the sickness and seeing him get stronger. My mind then turned dark and images of my time in jail flashed before me. The shock of hot tears streaming down my face snapped me out of my mental movie.

The cute flight attendant woke me up. "Sir, wake up. Sir?" Slowly I came out of my deep slumber, slurring my words: "Are we gonna land soon?" came out as unintelligible gibberish. He must have thought I was on drugs.

"Are you okay?" asked the flight attendant.

"Oh, sorry. Yes, thank you." Now a bit more awake, I noticed the plane was in a complete stop. I looked around. I was the last person on the plane! I grabbed my duffle bag and trudged off the plane.

I slogged through the long corridor like a zombie to get to baggage claim and noticed all these happy people meeting up with the other passengers from the flight. They were hugging and holding up signs. Everyone had someone waiting for them. Well, everyone but me. I felt lonely. Me against the world. I was ready to conquer it…wasn't I?

Sometimes my mind is like an angel and devil fighting one another. One of those inner shouting matches was just triggered as I realized: I'm here alone, with one beat up old suitcase, and no big game plan. The positive "I'm ready to conquer the world" was challenged by the insidious mocking whispers of "Dumb kid, this town will eat you alive." Everyone had already grabbed their bags and left. Here I was, last at the baggage carousel, picking up my one, lonely bag and wondering, "What next?" But I had to believe; this is just the start.

I felt a whole lot better hopping into a taxi and giving the driver a card with my hotel's name and address. Suddenly I felt not just better, but important. I closed my eyes as the glorious L.A. sun warmed my face. I imagined myself as some foreign diplomat in a stretch limousine being chauffeured to an elegant, ritzy hotel. Occasionally I'd open one eye for an instant and catch a glimpse of one of these elegant retreats for the rich; places so perfect in their refinement you never want to leave, and certainly not without one of their $300 hundred robes in your Tumi suitcase.

The taxi pulled up to my hotel. Correction: hostel. I'd forgotten that, weeks ago, in a moment of clarity, I booked myself here. Cheap! Twenty-four dollars a night. Cheap was essential. My savings wouldn't last long if I had problems finding work, or, as they say, if I got hit by a bus. I wasn't being overly cautious. I was in Los Angeles, the misnamed city. The city of angels it was not. In this city a lot of things could hit you like a bus.

So I'm standing like a flat-footed tourist in front of the Pineapple Bungalow. Could I get robbed here? Didn't look too safe. No need to panic; I just had a small suitcase with a change of clothes and shoes. I left most of my stuff with Sheldon back in Seattle, and the plan was that he would send them to me once I was settled in something more permanent.

This was not a place with fancy amenities; few guest services here. Bare bones, basic. The less-than-grand Pineapple Bungalow had a coin laundry and included free breakfast. Outside, there was a courtyard where people could play basketball, foosball, ping pong or take advantage of the free wi-fi.

Free.

Free!

When you're starting out, "free" is the greatest word in the English language. You'd think that "cheap" would be the second best word, right? Hold that thought until I mention something important: I'd forgotten that these cheap rooms were shared rooms. No privacy. I had roommates. Just as I thought it couldn't get any worse, I met my first roommate and wondered if it could get any better.

Jan was a 25-year-old gym rat from the Czech Republic. He was a personal trainer who was certified back in his country, but was now a student here trying to get his U.S. credentials. This guy had been busting his butt in the gym since he was 14 years old. At 6'5", his physique was a bodybuilder's dream … almost unreal and it was his personal advertising for his services.

This European stud had a great positive attitude. He was smart and had a touch of broken English that made him adorable. He'd been staying at the hostel for almost a month.

Only one small downside; he was straight. But this wasn't the YMCA and this wasn't the disco seventies. I considered myself lucky. Sex isn't everything.

We stayed in something they called the "Traveler Dorm Bed w/ Kitchen." It was a shared room with two other people. The small room had a bunk bed in one corner and a single bed on the other side. It also had a private bath, carpet, and a small kitchen, which included a microwave, stove, refrigerator, dining space, small television, and cooking and dining supplies.

My second roommate was 23-year-old Benjamin, also known as Ben, from Phoenix, Arizona. A 5'4" Puerto Rican, he was on the skinny side, with a tiny nose and black prescription glasses. Ben had a smile that seemed to be permanently etched on his face and a short buzzed head. He was a little guy with a big personality, also straight, and clearly addicted to getting tattoos. His big Los Angeles dream was to be a film director and editor, and he had been working on a project for the big L.A. film festival that was coming up. He'd been staying at the hostel almost as long as Jan.

Ben and I slept in the bunk beds while Jan slept in the

single bed. For the most part, we all got along well and stayed out of each other's way. During my time there, I got to know my roommates really well and I don't just mean that I saw them naked more than a few times. At night we'd share everything with each other, from our secrets to our fears. I learned a lot about those two and they did about me. They never once judged me or treated me different. I considered myself lucky to have them as my first friends here and I couldn't be happier. They both had their goals, their plans, and a solid determination to achieve them. I envied these guys. They were charting a roadmap to success. I was lost. If I didn't find my way soon, I would run out of money. Ready or not, my first plan was formed – make Los Angeles my bitch!

Chapter Two:

Roommate

Jan took a job as a full time trainer in North Hollywood. He quickly found a small apartment close by. Ben also moved away to the city of Long Beach, to film a small independent movie for five months.

After they moved away from the hostel, I knew I had to get myself together and figure something out. They had moved ahead. I was treading water, and every exhausted swimmer knows the water eventually wins.

The Pineapple Bungalow was a pretty neat place, but the best part of it was the internet room. I spent hours online applying to every single job that I could think of; from retail stores to restaurants, valet companies, catering companies, and even hotels. I did all of the job application forms online at the library computer.

And then I waited. And waited. Waiting in vain for someone to call me back for an interview.

I knew this town wasn't easy. What made it so hard to live here was the high cost of living. I realized I had to work even harder to stay above water.

Those two voices in my head, angelic and demonic, came back: "Maybe a little help from my parents isn't such a bad idea."

The second voice said, "Pussy!"

This time it was easy to know the angel from the devil. I'm no pussy. Time to show this town who I am.

For a week the phone never rang. Finally a few places I had applied to asked to speak to me. I took out my best formal clothing, printed out my resume and promised myself that I wouldn't come back without getting a job. Over the next couple of days, I went to four different interviews. From two of those I needed a follow-up interview.

Some of the interviewers seemed cold as ice, never cracked a smile, never showed any sign of encouragement. My confidence level? Running on empty. My wallet? Thinner and thinner.

I kept getting the same tired, formulaic answer when leaving the interviews: "We will let you know in a few days." A few days went by and I didn't hear a word. Sure, I had money in my pocket, but it wouldn't last forever. I was set up to last a year … possibly as long as two years, but only if I stretched every dollar. I needed a job so badly. I questioned myself; maybe I wasn't good at interviewing after all.

What was I going to do if I couldn't find a job? Then the clouds parted, and three of the jobs called back offering me work. I accepted all three. I would have mornings free, but most of my week would be packed with work. Mondays and Tuesdays I was a Valet driver. On Wednesdays and Thursdays, I wore my headphones and danced on the street with an arrow sign outside of a sandwich shop, and on Fridays and Saturdays, I was a doorman for a five-star hotel in Beverly Hills.

Next, I needed a car to get to all three jobs. I went to a used-car dealership and bought a 2006 Toyota Camry – a nice, used vehicle that was well taken care of and felt like a really smart buy. The car was my first big purchase, and I was mighty proud.

I had been saving up my money from working at all three of my jobs, so it was a good time to leave the hostel. After all, I couldn't live there forever, and paying for parking for my car at a nearby lot every night was getting expensive. I looked for rooms to rent in the online ads, searched in the newspaper and even asked my co-workers if they knew of someone looking for a roommate.

Through one of the online ads, I found a two-bedroom apartment that had a room for rent. The apartment was located in the middle of Chinatown – not exactly my first choice, but it was worth a look, given that it was dirt-cheap. I called the number on the ad, and a guy answered offering to show me his apartment. I drove over to the apartment complex and found a little light blue building with a dozen apartments inside. Kids were playing outside the building, which gave me the impression that most of the apartments were filled with families. Behind a noisy group of children, Shaun was waiting for me

Shaun was a sixty-year-old fashionable gay man – an English teacher with a somewhat grumpy character. Maybe grumpy is the wrong word ... Edgy? Ill-tempered? Huffy? It was hard to put a finger on this man's personality. He was nice enough, but every time he talked, his words seemed to have a double meaning or some sort of veiled insult within them. His insults were never towards me, but I found his attitude odd.

Case in point; while walking to the apartment, we passed his neighbor. Shaun asked, "Lola, how are you girl? Did you like the cake I baked you?"

She replied, "Absolutely yummy, thanks. I'll bring you back your plate later today." As soon as we were far enough away from Lola, Shaun opened up.

He whispered to me, "That girl is a mess. She has six kids, two baby-daddies, but no man in the house. How they all fit in a two-bedroom apartment is beyond me." I found him funny but a little bit bitchy. We walked all the way to the back of the building where his apartment was located.

His apartment was cramped and crowded inside. He had all kinds of Hollywood memorabilia and literally thousands upon thousands of books. The books ranged from literature to history, biography and photography; they were all over the living room. The walls were all framed with paintings and pictures of half-naked men.

There was a stack of old newspapers by the door and mini statues of freaky clowns everywhere.

In a span of just a few feet we went from dirty, claustrophobic clutter to a spic and span, spartan room; just a queen-sized bed and a big empty closet. It was even bigger than I thought it would be. It cost $300 a month including utilities, plus a parking spot.

He told me that he could use the extra money and that the room was mine if I wanted it. The price was right, and the room was great compared to everything else I had seen. I agreed to move in.

After a few days, I was all moved in to the apartment. Shaun began to slowly open up to me, sharing more and more about his story and revealing a lot about why he was the way he was. Shaun told me that he came from a small town in South Dakota. The people there laughed and teased him in school, long before he ever came out. Kids just found him weird, odd, and that anything different in his town was a target for ridicule, distrust, or even hatred.

When he was 15 years old, he took a tour of the nearby Air Force base and met many of the men and women who were stationed there. During the tour he slipped away to use the rest room.   He found himself peeing in one of those long, bathtub-looking urinals next to an airman. Shaun looked over at his dick, and next thing he knew, he was being raped in one of the stalls with a sock in his mouth.

After that, he became very sexually promiscuous. That behavior got him into trouble when he met up with a straight man pretending to be gay and was assaulted by the man and his friends. The beating almost put him in a coma, and he had been a little 'off' since then. He never found a life partner. As a result, he felt that his best years had escaped him and that no one would ever be interested in an old man. Lastly, he was a little bitter because he saw how much more acceptable homosexuality was now than it used to be … he felt cheated in life.

My daily schedule went something like this: I'd wake up, eat breakfast with Shaun, run to the gym, work out for a few hours, and then go to one of my many jobs. And when I got back close to midnight every night, Shaun was waiting for me, wanting to talk about my day. He always offered to give me a foot rub (I never accepted) and often had dinner ready for me. He was such a lonely soul and always wanted to hang out on the weekends when I had time off. I didn't mind spending time with him, but after a while, it was getting to be too much. He wanted to have all of my spare time, as I was his only "friend."

His favorite topic was himself. He talked about nothing except gossip about his co-workers, complaining about his students, and had a terrible case of a low self-esteem. He would use it as a form of manipulation to try to get a stream of compliments and reassurance out of me. "Do you think I look too fat?" and "Why don't people like me?" were asked over and over, as if he hoped each time to get a more flattering response.

He was always fishing for compliments and secretly wanting me to rush in with the classic, "Oh no, you're not fat, you're gorgeous!" or "Of course people like you. Why wouldn't they?" He wanted positive answers and reinforcement. It was emotionally draining.

One time, I caught Shaun outside my bedroom, holding on to the doorframe, peeking through with his crazy eyes, watching me sleep. It really freaked me out and rubbed me the wrong way. How long had he been standing there? Even worse, I always closed my door at night. So why was it open? Once he saw that I was awake, he just said, "Good morning, sunshine ... breakfast is ready." Not really knowing what to say I just said, "I'll be right out."

I got out of bed and jumped into the shower. I felt so weirded out and for some reason really dirty. I kept scrubbing and scrubbing my body with the loofah. What have I gotten myself into? Something needed to change.

Chapter Three:

Modeling

I woke up early one Saturday morning, put on shorts and running sneakers, and headed out the door. I drove to Runyon Canyon to hike, clear my mind, meditate, and maybe even pray a little. I was at a point where I was just asking God for some guidance. I also needed a much needed break from Shaun and all his negativity and weirdness. I dreaded going home.

Under the warm sun, I sat down on my shirt and just bathed in the rays. Suddenly, a guy in his late 30s came up to me on the top of the hill. He was also shirtless, wearing only cargo shorts and from the look of it, no underwear. He stood about 6'2" and was a light-skinned black guy. He was muscular – built like a house, with piercing green eyes and an amazing face with strong features.

The brown-skinned Adonis' name was Mark. After the typical introductions he apologized for interrupting my prayers.

"Religious?"

"You can say that..."

"Oh, well, sorry to disturb your praying, but I have a quick question for you, and then I'll be on my way..."

"Sure."

"Are you in the great business we call 'Show Business'?"

"No I'm not. Why do you ask?"

"Man, you should be. I don't usually do this, but I am a co-owner of a large modeling agency here in Los Angeles. You would be perfect."

"Modeling? I don't know..."

"You've taken pictures haven't you?"

"Not professionally."

"Well … it's the same idea. Just try not to blink! I'm kidding – it's a bit harder work than that, but you have natural beauty and the height. I have a feeling that you'd do well in this job, and my feelings are never wrong. How tall are you?"

"I'm 6'1", but I don't know about your 'feeling.'"

In the back of my mind I thought two things: one, it's all bull, or two, he's a crazy creeper trying to get in my pants. And if that was the case, I might let him. He was gorgeous and it had been over a year since I'd gotten laid!

"You have nothing to lose and everything to gain," he prodded.

"I guess so..."

"Well, think about it. I'd love to represent you. Here is my card," he finished, handing me his business card and punctuating his solicitation by telling me I could be his next great discovery.

"Thanks Mark. I'll think about it."

After that day I kept thinking about what Mark said. I wasn't sure if he was right about being a big discovery, but he was right in one thing: there is no harm in trying. But what if he was a fake? I had to Google him to see if he was the real deal. Surprisingly, he wasn't lying. The website I came across showed pictures of beautiful men and women who were represented by his agency. They looked too good to be true; these were incredible specimens. I couldn't see myself in that list. But maybe Mark saw something in me that I didn't. It was worth a try. Maybe this was the sign I had been asking God to provide.

I gave him a call, and he seemed happy to hear from me. We set up a meeting time in his office and talked things over. He first took a few quick Polaroid's of me to see how well I photographed. Serious concern was written all over his face. He told me he needed to try something else, changed angle and lighting, and began fresh.

I desperately wanted to see the photos, but he was too busy and professional to interrupt.

Then he put the camera down. No poker face on this guy. He was very candid about what he thought and wasn't too shy to say it.

In his opinion, even though I had solid good looks, I was only marginally photogenic.

"Don't be too disappointed. It's just the quirky nature of photography."

"It's okay. I never thought of myself as a model anyway."

"Ironically a lot of people who look completely average, people you see every day walking down the street or in the supermarket look amazing on film. It's a crazy business."

I gathered my things and was ready to say goodbye, but his co-workers were buzzing in a heated, private conversation with him in the next room. Were they poking fun at me?

Mark caught me before I could slip out the door.

"My co-workers think this is a democracy and have out-voted me. I'm sending you to Robby."

"Who is Robby?"

I was soon to find out who Robby was, but first they needed me to sign a piece of paper: a modeling contract… for me! It all seemed surreal. Not me. How many times did my father say only my brother inherited his good looks?

The agency put together a mini job for me. It paid next-to-nothing, but it was a plain and simple one that would be a good start for my career, if I indeed had a career. That hadn't been decided. Those insidious cameras would either make me look like model material or not, and from what I understood, it was all up to Robby to perform his magic.

I was to do mostly head shots, but also a few shirtless pictures, either in jeans or just underwear. When I got to the photographer's small studio downtown, there was a table with a few cameras, memory cards, lenses, photo books of recent work and a computer. It was all extremely organized. Everything had its place, neatly stacked and just inches apart on the table. I thought this photographer might have a small case of OCD. But where was he? I looked around and suddenly heard a voice behind me.

"So you must be Roberto," he said.

"That's me," I responded.

"I'm Robby."

Robby, so this is the guy. The way they talked about him, I thought he'd fly in on a shaft of light, surrounded by angels. I wanted to make a good impression. What could I say that would make a good impression, that sounded witty?

"Nice to meet you," was all I could manage.

"Same here. Ready to work?"

"Yes sir. Ready!"

Great. Now I sounded like some over-eager bumpkin who just got off the Greyhound bus from rural Idaho.

"Nervous?"

"It's my first shoot." He understood what that meant: petrified.

"You'll do fine. I like your look, so should be a fairly easy shoot."

"Oh, good to hear." Already he was making me feel more at ease.

Robby told me that he was a bit old-fashioned and would be shooting with a film camera. If he liked the pictures, I would be part of a gallery show he was putting together a few weeks from then. That meant the possibility of being paid more … maybe a lot more.

So, I got quick haircut and they put a bit of makeup on me. They told me they wanted to keep it a bit natural, and that I didn't need much anyway.

"You have to tell me your secret. What do you use to keep your skin so flawless" the stylist asked me.

"Basically all-natural, organic products."

This wasn't a complete lie. Water is natural and organic, isn't it? But beyond that, and some soap, I didn't use anything.

"It helps to have perfect skin, because when you are shooting in film, our work is raw and unedited. What we shoot is what we will get," Robby said.

"Great!"

The shoot was about to start and my nerves kicked in. "Hopefully I can do this," I told myself. My shirt came off. I was standing there wearing only jeans, waiting to be photographed. I was in this box-like area with two flash screens on both sides of me and white paper behind me as a background that ran down to my feet. Robby began to check his lighting and was ready to begin.

"Don't be nervous," he said. "Just relax; don't think of this as a job. Just try and be natural, nothing forced."

"Okay."

I think he saw I was still a bit lost and said, "What I mean is ... don't try to act sexy. You are good-looking on your own. That comes naturally. It's the emotion and story you are trying to give through your eyes that I'm trying to capture."

"Okay."

"Today I want you to give me ... sadness, tough and serious, and innocence."

"Got it."

And Robby went to work. At first, the whole thing was awkward, and I felt uncomfortable. But that feeling quickly went away. It wasn't that hard once I cleared my thoughts and doubts and just focused on the task. I just stopped thinking and went along with what I felt during his direction. I gave him his emotions, and from what he told me, he got exactly what he wanted. He thanked me for the shoot and told me that he would print out the pictures and see how they looked. He also said that if they came out how he thought they would, I was definitely going to be featured in his gallery show.

Not so many years ago I was a kid with crooked teeth and acne, and now they want to hang my photographs in a gallery? On top of this, they really think people will buy them?

Robby gave my agency great reviews about my performance the next day. I didn't know if it was sincere or if he felt sorry for a nervous kid with no experience. I received an invitation to go to the gallery show.

My roommate Shaun had been a nightmare all week. Clearly he needed to get out if his mood was to improve, so I invited him to come along.

When we arrived at the gallery, the room was filled with maybe between 60 and 70 people. This didn't give us much space to move around. Everyone had a drink in their hand – they were socializing, eating appetizers, and looking at all the big black and white pictures that were framed and hung around the room. But I could not see mine yet.

"God everyone looks so stuck up," said Shaun.

"Try to have fun," I responded sharply.

"I'll try …" he replied, rolling his eyes.

Shaun and I walked around the room looking at all the framed pictures. We came to an abrupt halt in front of the picture with my giant face. I couldn't believe what I was looking at. It was a surreal moment. Robby chose the head-on picture of me where I was looking sorrowful. There was even a tear in my eye about to drop down my cheek. I must have been too into my character, because I didn't remember crying. Overall, it was actually a beautiful picture – very angelic, natural and sad. It definitely told a story. There was also a red little sticker in the bottom next to the frame, which meant that it had been sold. The price was shocking. It went for $3,000!

"Wow, someone overpaid," said Shaun.

"I would disagree," said Robby, appearing behind us.

"Hey Robby, nice to see you," I said. I hugged him and whispered, "Sorry about my friend."

"It's okay," he whispered back. "Nice to see you Roberto, and your friend, too."

"No offense. Just my opinion," Shaun added, prodding further.

"It's a good thing you might be the only one in the room to think that way, or I'd never sell any again," Robby said, trying to lighten the mood.

"Lucky you," Shaun bit back.

Robby turned his attention toward me: "Yeah … So Roberto, what do you think of your picture?"

"I love it. You did great making me look good."

"Well it was easy with you. I hardly did a thing. I just captured you by clicking the button. Without you, it's nothing but a background."

"That's nice of you to say."

"It's the truth. Oh and by the way ... you also get this." He handed me a small book.

"Wow, I'm on the cover of your gallery book too?"

"Yeah, you earned it. This is your copy."

"Thank you so much! It's an honor."

"Well, it was my pleasure, and your agency will be giving you a nice bonus too. I have to go mingle now. I hope you both enjoy yourself."

And with a hug, he went away into the crowd. The rest of the evening went very well. People kept stopping me to take a picture with them, with my big picture in the background. Shaun, however, had a sour face the whole night and wasn't impressed. I swore to myself that was the last time I would invite him anywhere!

After that job, I just started building my photographer rolodex one by one. The more I started going to auditions, the more work I received. One job led to another, and soon, I was starting to get somewhat well known. I worked with some well-known photographers, and some of the most beautiful people (both men and women) I'd ever seen, I did small ads and spreads in magazines, worked with a variety of styles from fitness to fashion, landed a few big music videos, started doing runway shows, and eventually got to the point where I was in a few really big underwear and cologne campaigns.

A few more agencies signed me up in New York, London, Paris, Milan, and Tokyo (I was big in Tokyo). The travel was difficult but also very exciting, and the paychecks kept getting bigger and bigger. The money really surprised me, but I started to hear that I was considered a male "supermodel." This was what many people dream of.

Beyond that, people really liked me. I didn't understand why. I guess deep down, I knew why I didn't see what others saw in me. It was the result of being mentally beat down by my father for all those years as a kid. Thanks to him, I still saw myself as the ugly duckling. It was a battle in my mind to tell myself that I was good enough. I felt very, very lucky, but I still never took the job too seriously. I knew that looks eventually fade, so I always saw it as a fun and really well paid hobby.

What did I want to be "when I grew up?" That was the real question. I was still figuring that out, and I decided that I'd ride the modeling wave and save my money for as long as I could … or until I figured out who and where I wanted to be.

Chapter Four:

Twins

I woke up extra early one Tuesday morning because I had a full day ahead of me. My agency had booked me for this group sports-type sexy photo shoot to promote new running shoes. I arrived at the running-track location an hour-and-a-half early. The photographer wasn't even there yet; only the crew guys setting up. So I waited on the side bleachers until it was time to get to "work."

When I realized that the shoot was with these two hot, muscular and straight twins, I was very happy. I was familiar with their work. Their names were Jacob and Joshua – 23 years old with ripped, eight-pack abs, bright white smiles, black earrings, full and plumped pink lips, short dark brown hair, and dark brown eyes. They were mixed race – half-black and half-Mexican. I was instantly interested in them. I wanted both! And maybe at the same time! Well, I'd settle for at least one. The crew pointed to me, and the twins walked toward the bleachers.

They both came over and introduced themselves to me with their sexy confident voices. "So you must be the other model," they said.

"That's me. I'm Roberto."

"Joshua."

"Jacob." Both said their names at the same time.

"Want to warm up with me? I'm going run around for a few," I asked them as I took out my old track shoes.

"Great idea!" they both said.

"You brought your own shoes?" Jacob asked.

"Yup. My old track shoes."

"So did we," said Joshua

"So you ran track and field too?" asked Joshua.

"I did. Ran hurdles and relays."

"Awesome! Our kind of guy. We did the 100, 400, and 800." said Jacob

"Cool. My kind of guys too. So, you ready? Try and keep up, guys." They laughed, put their shoes on and followed me down to the track.

After a few laps, we were all warmed up, and they called us in to start shooting. We all had to wear just shorts, socks and the running shoes. They oiled us up and made us run a few times for the action shots. We took turns doing that for hours in several different shoes and shorts. Then we stood together for the group shot. It was very sexy, sporty and playful, but still with a very "straight" look. It gave me shocks through my body when one of them would touch their chest to my skin. Overall, I think we made a good trio, and we took some good pictures for the brand. By the end of the day they both ended up giving me their phone numbers. They wanted to hang and maybe be my running buddies. I was all for that. I tried not to sound too excited when I gave them my digits.

The day after the shoot, I got a text message from Jacob.

"Hey Roberto, busy?"

"Not at the moment. Just finished my workout. What's up?" I replied.

"I'm in your neighborhood. Want to hang out?"

"Sure, what do you want to do?"

"Up for anything. Do you own any good movies? Pizza?

"A whole library of movies and I can order some pizza."

He came over 30 minutes later, parked his car right in front of the apartment complex, gave me a hug, and I handed him the permit so he wouldn't get ticketed or towed.

"Hey Jacob, how are you?" I asked as I greeted him.

"I'm pretty good. Just a bit frustrated. I can't believe how bad traffic is here in LA. We don't have it this bad back home."

"Where are you from?" I asked.

"We moved here from a small town in Indiana."

"Oh I see. I guess that is a big change." He walked with me into the apartment. It was as clean as it could be but the best part was that my grumpy roommate was out of town.

"Nice place you have here. Cool location, too, I like China town." he said.

"Thank you. My roommate is a big collector. "

"Oh, is he here?" He asked.

"No, he's visiting his family out of state."

I don't know if it's my own insecurities, but when I hang around straight guys, my guard goes way up, and I tend to "butch it up" a bit more. Before I was out, I didn't really think about it much, mostly because I didn't know any other gay people. I used to be fine, but now that I mostly have gay friends around, straight people seem to be the outcasts. I feel like he wouldn't like me if he knew. But wait, I thought … does he know? Why is he being so nice? Is this normal? I was just going to go along with it and just be as friendly as a "straight man" can be.

I lead him to my room, where my television and dvd collection was.

"So, what do you want to watch?" I asked.

"Not sure. What are the options?" he responded. I pointed to my library on the side wall by the restroom.

"I have literally hundreds of titles to choose from. It's a lot, I know." He went over and started looking.

"Nice selections you have here. Some I haven't heard of. Is Priscilla -- Queen of the Desert good?" Oh shit, I thought … I forgot about my gay cinema! Now he really knows I'm gay.

"It's pretty good, but maybe pick something with action … or scary would be good. I'm in one of those moods," I said as I deflected him away from the gay movies.

So he pops in the movie of his choice while I made the popcorn. He chose a scary movie and sat on the beanbag chair, so I took the twin bed across the room. The television was in the middle facing us. I gave him the popcorn, and after a while, he started playfully throwing some across the room for me to catch with my mouth. The movie kept playing, but throughout the movie he would make small comments like, "Oh wow she's a hottie," or ,"Great, now I won't be able to fall asleep," or, "A Disney movie sounds good right about now." When it was finally over, it was a bit late. He was stretching his arms over his head and yawning, and without thinking, the words came out of my mouth:

"You can sleep over here if you are too tired to drive and don't mind the sleeping bag"

"Sad, you aren't offering the bed?"

"I don't like you that much!" I laughed.

"This how you treat your guests?"

"I'm kidding. I'll take the sleeping bag if you want my bed."

"No, the floor is fine, thank you. I'm too tired to drive back."

I got undressed down to my boxers and put away my clothes.

"Do you have any shorts I could borrow?" he asked. I gave him some shorts to sleep in, and out of the corner of my eye, I watched him undress in front of me. It was unreal. His body was perfectly sculpted and that skin was a perfect tan. God definitely took his time making this perfect specimen. I turned off the lights and said good night. I was not tired. How could I be with this hottie only a few feet away from me? I had the biggest boner. I kept tossing and turning. I tried to clear my head but it wasn't working so I tried counting sheep, thought of the list of things I needed to do the next day, I even told myself a story in my head … but nothing was working.

One hour passed, then two, then three and I was still wide awake. It got annoying. I got up trying not to make any noise so I wouldn't wake Jacob up. He was faced down showing only his strong back. I went to the kitchen and drank a glass of water. Then went to the restroom and sat on the toilet for a bit, just killing time, flipping through magazines and reading some articles. When I finally felt I was getting a bit tired, I headed back to my bed.

When I was under the covers I heard his voice ask, " You can't sleep?"

"Oh, sorry, I didn't mean to wake you. Yeah, I can't seem to."

"It's cool. I can't either. I've been trying for hours," he said.

"Yeah! It sucks man."

"I've tried nearly every trick I can think of. Nothing is working," he said.

"Me too. Wait, nearly every trick?" I decided to dig a little deeper.

"Yeah."

"What haven't you tried?"

"Well to be honest, what always does the trick is jerking off or having sex."

"Oh." I was surprised, but didn't know what else to say. "Well go ahead."

"Nah, it would be embarrassing."

"I don't mind. I won't look. Unless you want to keep staying up all night."

There was a long pause, but he finally managed to say, "Jerking off alone is weird. Do it with me."

My heart stopped or started beating in a super slow motion speed!

"I'm down," I responded.

"Really?"

"Yeah, I'm not shy."

"Fuck it."

Even though the lights were off in my room, some soft light was coming in through the window from the outside giving us just enough where we could see each other clearly. I took off my underwear and threw them on the floor, leaving me completely naked under the covers. He did the same. I began to slowly play with Aaron (my penis), and he then followed my lead. I tried so hard to focus on only myself but I couldn't help and look over to see the sheet get lower and lower down his body as he stroked. When I say this guy was sculpted, it's an understatement. He had ripple after ripple of muscle. Besides his beautiful symmetrical face and big chest, I counted eight-pack abs, but they looked more like ten. He seriously had no body fat. It was the perfect jerking-off material. I felt more and more comfortable, mostly because this didn't seem real. It was more like a fantasy. Maybe I did fall asleep and I was dreaming. I got so comfortable that my sheet was down to my ankles and I was fully exposed.

"Wow, you have a big dong," he said

"Thanks man. I haven't had any complaints yet." He laughed. "Well from what I can see, you are pretty huge yourself." I added.

"I'm decent."

"No, really. It's a good tool you have there."

"Thank you."

He was around 9 inches cut … veiny and dark skinned with huge hangers. He was oozing pre-cum. He was so turned on. I got ballsy and decided to take this a step further.

"Can I see it closer?"

"Sure … if you want."

I walked over the few feet we were apart and was standing right in front of it. It looked even better closer. I felt saliva gathering in my mouth, like I was a starving lion being teased with a piece of steak. I had to go for it.

"May I?"

"Okay."

I went to work, from hand to mouth. He moaned and moaned, saying things like, "oh, fuck!" and "that so feels good."

After a while, he screamed, "Oh, my God!" and he creamed hard all over himself. I turned over and creamed on myself. He was a bit too quiet, so I got up and handed him a towel. He cleaned up his juice off his abs, and as he handed me back the dirty towel, he finally said, "Well, now I'll be sleeping like a baby. I'm beat."

"Me too. Good night"

"'Night."

It was early the next morning and his watch alarm went off, waking us up. I had a big smile on my face because he was still completely naked and so was I. It wasn't a dream!

"I feel like shit," he said.

"Me too. I could have used more sleep."

"Sorry, I've got to go meet my brother and my friends. We always run for an hour around the track in the mornings, and I'm already late but it's close by."

"Oh, okay."

He got up from the floor, and the white sheet fell off showing his naked body. He couldn't find his underwear. We both searched for it, though occasionally the focus of my attention was on his sculpted body as he knelt, bent and twisted, looking everywhere for the missing underwear. Finally, just as one delicious bead of sweat ran down his back, he extricated them from under a pillow carelessly thrown on the floor.

We got dressed, and I walked him back to his car. My guest parking permit was still there and he gave it back to me. I wished him a good day, and he hugged me. Ten minutes later I get a text message from him.

"Wow, that was ... interesting."

"Yeah, it was," I responded. "Sorry. It wasn't my evil plan to get you naked."

"It's okay. It wasn't bad actually. I'm a big boy. I made the decision. Just don't say anything."

"Sure."

A few days after my fun with Jacob, his twin brother Joshua texted me. It was 1:00 am.

"Are you still up?" he asked.

"Yeah. Can't sleep. What's up?"

"Bored. Want to chat online? Any messenger?"

"Sure."

We exchanged information, and when he popped online, next to his screen name his status said, "Horny. Taking care of business."

"You there?" he messaged me.

"Yeah. What's up with your status?"

"Oh I forgot I had that up. I should change that. Well... Maybe not. I'm kind of in the same situation now. LOL!"

"Really?"

"Yeah … it's been a long day. I need to unload one."

"Well go and do that and get back to me. I'll probably go and do the same thing. It might help me sleep."

"You horny too?"

"Yeah, kinda."

"I don't believe you."

"I am. Why wouldn't I be?"

"I don't know."

"Well I am."

"Prove it." Oh shit, I thought ...did he just say that? I had just messed around with his brother, and now Joshua is hitting on me. Wow, I guess both are gay ...or at least gay enough.

"How?" I asked.

"I don't know. Turn on your cam."

"Alright, but you got to do it too."

"Okay." I turned on my cam. I only had underwear on and I had one light on in front of me. He then turned on his, and even though it was dark and difficult to see, I could tell he had a full hard on. And his dick was the same size and same appearance as his brother's.

"Wow. I didn't know it was going to be that kind of a show," I said.

"Sorry."

"Why is it so dark over there? Let me see your face and turn a light on." He got up, turned on the light, and I saw his amazing cut body. His face was now in front of the camera.

"Better?" he asked.

"Much."

"Horny?"

"Very."

He showed me himself playing with his not-so-little soldier. It was extremely hot. We both went at it for a good 30 minutes until we both exploded on our stomachs.

He said, "That was hot. Let's do it again sometime."

"Sure."

Then he ended the conversation with, "Please don't tell anyone about it. Let's keep it our secret."

"Okay," I added.

Maybe in time a threesome would be possible, and I would get my wish to have them both at the same time … and, no, I'm not talking about double penetration! What a dirty thought! It might not happen, since both are big closet cases.

Over the next few days, they both became more and more distant. I'd get a random text message every now and then wanting to mess around, but at that point, I just said no. Honestly, confused men are more of a turn off than anything.

Chapter Five:

Supermodel

I met William through a photographer friend of mine. He had seen some of my pictures and apparently was smitten by me. William is an American supermodel and is a few years older than me. He has been on many covers and spreads, in campaigns and films, and has walked runways for many great designers. When I got the text message that he wanted to hang out, it was surprising.

"Roberto?" it read.

"Who's asking?" I responded to the number.

"William here."

At first I didn't know who it was, but only one William came to mind, and that was the model.

"The model?" I asked.

He laughed and said "Yeah, that's me."

"Oh, hello. What's up? How did you get my number? Stalking me?"

"Very funny. I actually stole your phone number from a photographer friend of ours. Hope you don't mind. Wow, I guess that is a little stalker-ish." He said.

He had a great personality and sounded very charming over the phone. He told me that he lived in Florida but was visiting LA for a modeling job and wanted to hang out. Of course I wasn't going to say no to one of the hottest guys in the modeling world. So we agreed to go out for dinner and watch a movie. I couldn't believe it; I was going to go on a real date with William!

He picked me up around 9:00 pm at my apartment in his nice rental car: a black Audi. When he got out of the car, it was like I was watching a superstar. I had never seen someone as handsome as him. He was 28 years old, 6'2" with Pacific-blue eyes, short blonde hair, wearing a tight yellow polo shirt that showed off his swimmer's build, perfect chest, and the ripples of his eight pack. What drove me crazy was his nice juicy pink lips and the scruff of facial hair. He walked towards me and gave me a hug, then opened the car door for me.

We went to a Mexican restaurant that was a few blocks away from my place. I ordered the food for us at the counter, and he was impressed with my Spanish.

"God, you are sexy," he said after the server had walked away. William had a way with words where he would just make me feel like I was the hottest man alive. We took our trays with food and talked about almost everything. He wanted to hold my hand under the table. It was great to hang with someone so down-to-earth.

Then I took him to this old run-down building. From the outside, it looked like any other building in the area. It had big black windows and was eight floors high.

"Where are you taking me?" he asked.

"It's a surprise," I told him. We entered the building. The first floor was like a mini mall or a swap meet but everything was closed. He was so confused. We turned a few corners to go up the elevator. I pushed the button for the fourth floor and waited.

"Really, where are you taking me? This is like a tiny Chinatown. It's a whole other world over here."

"Just wait and see." The doors opened, and we were greeted by a long hall with bright red and yellow walls, movie posters, a ticket window and a concession stand at the end of the hall. The whole floor was a hidden movie theater. He was very surprised and had a big smile on his face.

"How did you know about this place?" he asked.

"I know people." I grabbed our movie tickets to the next movie playing – an animated film. When we got in the theater, it was completely empty. It was only 10:00 pm, but given that not many people know about this place, and it was an animated film, I figured we'd have it to ourselves. We took our seats all the way in the back of the movie theater right under the small window. We kept talking about our lives and his shoot here in Los Angeles, and then one Chinese couple came in with popcorn, soda, and candy. They flashed us a smile, a small wave, and sat right in the front part of the theater. Sitting next to William gave me a good feeling, and not just in my pants. He took my hand and held it in between our seats. He had a funny way of making you feel special. It was very romantic.

"Do you mind if I hold your hand?" he asked, long after he'd already grabbed it.

"No, I like it." I told him.

Soon the movie started playing, and I tried very hard to pay attention, but he made it difficult.

"You are so good looking. Maybe you're out of my league, man," he whispered in my ear.

I looked at him and said, "You are in a league of your own, man. I've never met anyone as handsome as you."

"You are too sweet. I'm glad we're going out."

Before I could even respond he looked deep into my eyes and whispered, "Is it bad that I want to kiss you?"

"Not at all."

I was so nervous that I tried to play it cool. "I don't know …you might be bad at it. But I'll risk it."

He smiled. "You jerk," he said as he leaned in to kiss me. He was not bad at all. Soft lips pressed against mine, and he was not too wet or aggressive. It was perfect … so romantic.

"Okay. So you aren't terrible."

"Thank you. You too. You are making me excited." He took the hand he was holding and placed it in between his legs. I could feel his penis fully erect. He was a decent, average size – around seven inches.

"Wow, all that from a kiss?" Now I was starting to get excited.

"Yeah, you are that good."

The fun didn't stop there. We were so caught up in the passionate kissing that crazy, stupid things just started to happen without us even thinking about it. He first unzipped my pants and I unzipped his. Our hands went down each other's pants while we were still kissing. He wasn't wearing any underwear. The feeling of his hand was amazing. Then I took off his pants, and I took off mine too. I slouched down a little and his head just automatically went straight down into my lap. My eyes started to wander around. I looked at the movie playing and at the couple in the front of the theatre. I kept watch while he worked my cock. He stayed there a long time, and I could tell he was enjoying himself. I stripped off his shirt. He was now completely naked, with just his pants around his ankles.

After a good time, he got up and said, "I want you in me."

"Sure. Do you want to go back to my place?"

"No, I can't wait," he begged.

He got up from the floor and got on my lap. He was rubbing his ass on me.

"Right here? Are you sure?" I asked.

"Yeah. I want it." I looked through my wallet for a condom but couldn't find it.

"Do you have one?" I asked.

"No, you don't?"

"No. We should stop."

"I don't want to." He bent over leaning over the seat in front of him. This was insane. Were we really doing this? I couldn't resist. The wild, horny animal inside me came out, and I could not stop myself. I ate him out for a few minutes, and he had a special gift of having a self-lubricating anus. That made our next step much easier. He slowly went lower and lower, making my "Aaron" disappear. He felt so good. I admit that he wasn't the tightest, but nonetheless, it felt amazing. We did our best to keep quiet. The harder I thrust into him, small moans came out of his mouth, but it wasn't enough to overpower the sound of the movie. I kept looking down to see if the couple would look up, but they didn't.

After a good amount of time massaging his prostate, I was ready to explode. I let out a small moan, and I released my seed inside him. He got off me and we put our clothes back on and in perfect timing the movie was over. He went straight to the bathroom to clean up a little. As I washed my hands, I thought to myself that it wasn't very smart having unprotected sex, but it was too late now, and damn … was it hot! We headed to the elevator and then towards the parking lot. When we got to his car he again opened my door and started driving me back to my apartment. We were both still a little shocked with what happened that we didn't say much on the ride back.

When we got to my apartment complex he said, "Can I come in for a second?"

"Sure. Just for a second. My roommate will be home in a few." He was so magnetic. He held my hand as we walked into my building. We went up the back stairs, and halfway up, he stopped me. He started kissing me, unzipped my pants and again wanted to play with Aaron. He licked and sucked like it was dinner. Man, was he good. Why couldn't I control myself around him? I stopped him and we headed up to my apartment.

As soon as we walked through the door he wanted to use the restroom, so I showed him the door and waited in my room. He was taking a while to come out, so I went to go check on him. I knocked on the door but when I did the door opened and I saw him washing his hands.

"Everything okay in here?"

"Yeah. Just taking my time. Thinking."

"Thinking? About what?"

"How fun that was. Never done anything like that before." That feeling of uncontrollable horniness came back to me again. He was so beautiful, leaning against the sink, looking at me with his bright blue eyes. I couldn't control myself.

"Want to do something for me?" I asked.

"Anything"

"I want to see you pleasure yourself."

He quickly pulled down his pants and boy was he already excited.

He ran his hands down his body until he reached his crotch. He began to pleasure himself, both slow and fast. It was a great sight. He bit his lip while stroking, and I could tell he was enjoying the show he was putting on for me, just not as much as I did. To my surprise, watching him do it made me orgasm in my pants without even touching myself!

"Did you just?" he asked.

"Yeah."

"Wow. Hot!"

"Yeah. That was a first."

Then we heard a door open, and William pushed me out of the bathroom. It was my roommate, but he was too drunk from going out that he just waved to me and went straight to his room. It was almost midnight, and I had a full agenda the next day. I wanted to keep playing with Mister Hottie, but I knew I had to say good night.

After William came out of the bathroom, I told him,

"Well it's getting late handsome. I'd like to hang some more but I need to get some sleep tonight, and with you around, I'm sure I won't get any."

"Yeah, me too. I've got to get going. Walk me to my car?" We got to his car and made out for a few more minutes. His arms were around my waist the whole time.

"I had fun."

"I did too. Have a good flight tomorrow," I said.

"Good night handsome."

He then got on his car and drove away.

I guess I can cross out fucking a male supermodel at a Chinese movie theater off my list.

Chapter Six:

Problem

As fun as it was having my thing with William, it was a bit disappointing because it was hard not to get attached so quickly with someone as handsome and as sweet as him. My feelings for him changed when I found out that he had a rich, 70-year-old husband back home. I found out because a few weeks later, I got a call from William's cell that was actually his husband yelling at me.

"Who the fuck is this?" he bellowed.

"Who's this?" I replied.

"I'm his man." There was a moment of icy silence.

"What?"

"Yeah, I'm his husband. Are you that slut named Roberto who he slept with in Los Angeles?"

"What the … I'm Roberto, but I'm no slut."

"We've been together for 6 years! I might be 70 years old and understand that shit happens, but I don't plan on sharing him again. Not with you, and not with anyone."

"Um, okay …"

"How dare you sleep with my man!"

"First of all, your man didn't tell me he was taken. So maybe you should be taking your anger out on him and not on me."

I was about to hang up when I hear him say, " I have. You should probably know that you might be infected with HIV after sleeping with him. I've been HIV positive for years and so is he."

I felt numb … dead. I was in so much shock that I went ice cold.

"I don't believe you. Let me talk to William." He handed the phone over to his husband … my one-night lover.

"Hello?" he said. I could tell he was crying.

"Is it true?" I asked.

"Yeah. I'm sorry."

"Sorry? Why didn't you tell me?"

"I don't know what to say. Forgive me." And with that, he hung up the phone.

I stood there frozen, holding the phone to my ear. I fell to the ground, and I cried for hours and hours. Thank God my roommate Shaun was out of town. I could not handle explaining myself to him. Oh my God, I thought … I could be HIV positive.

The next day, I went to my local Gay and Lesbian Center because I knew that they did HIV testing there. I had to know. I walked through the doors and went up to the third level where they dealt with health and treatment. I put my name on the list and was handed forms to fill out. After all the forms were done, I waited my turn. Looking around the waiting area, I noticed people were not making eye contact and keeping to themselves. I guess no one really wants to be seen or be noticed there. It was such an uncomfortable process, and it only got worse when they called me into a little examination room.

Doctor Rex wasn't like any doctor I had seen before. He was very cool-looking guy. Beneath his teal-green scrubs, I could see colorful tattoos on both buff arms. Around 6'1" tall, he was slim and athletic. I could tell he worked out. He had a light blue eye and a green eye, broad and strong eyebrows, small silver hoop earrings, an angular jaw, square shaped forehead, big full lips that gave mischievous grin, a long decisive nose and an over-the-top skinny, curled handlebar stache! This might have been an easier process if he wasn't such a cute pirate.

He began to ask me some questions about my sexual history: things like the number of partners I have had, if I'd I slept with anyone in the porn industry recently or had unprotected sex. I was honest with my answers and told him everything. I told him why I was there and that this was my first time ever being tested. It was an embarrassing conversation but it had to be done. He was very sweet about it and tried to make me feel as comfortable as he could. He took a Q-tip and wiped it inside my mouth to collect some saliva. He came back in just 20 minutes later with the result in his hand. When the word "positive" came out his mouth, the whole world went silent. I could see his lips moving, but I heard nothing more. Then, all of the sudden, the whole world went dark.

I woke up on the floor to his face on top of me trying to fan some air with his hands.

"Are you okay?" he asked. I looked at him with what seemed like giant tear drops coming down my face. I tried to say, "I'm fine," but not a word came out of me. It was like my voice had run away from me.

"Roberto, take a sip of water and try to sit up." As I drank the glass of water, I kept thinking, "Why me?" This is something that happens to other people. It can't happen to me. It just can't. What would my parents say now? One of their biggest fears when I came out to them was that I was going to get the "gay disease." How was my life going to be now? What would I do? Suicidal thoughts came to my head again, and I hate that. It was like that little monster that had been on my shoulder, trying to take the easy way out again. I'm stronger than this, I told myself … "get it together."

"Roberto, are you okay?"

"I think so."

"Good. I know this is not something that's easy, but you have to keep your head on straight and see what your options are."

"Okay. You are right. What do I do now?"

He told me that if the rapid test is positive, it is still necessary to send blood to a laboratory for a Western blot to be sure the rapid test result is correct.

"Let's start with that and we'll go from there," he said.

"Sure. Let's do that." He took my blood for testing and told me he would get back to me with the results in a few days.

"Stay positive, no pun intended," he told me. I think he could tell that I could use a hug, and he went ahead and gave it to me.

"Thanks, Doc."

"I'll give you a call when the results are ready." And out the door I went.

Waiting to hear back from the doctor was like standing in 110-degree desert heat, dying of thirst right in front of a soda machine, knowing you have no money. When the phone rang three days later from the Gay and Lesbian Center, my mind was already made up. I was determined to fight … to fight for my life. If this is the situation I am in now, then I'd have to deal with it. I mean, being HIV-positive isn't something to be proud of, I guess, but I'd have to keep telling myself that it's no longer a death sentence. People living with this disease do live long and healthy lives now. There is better treatment out there. I know I can get through this. Now I just had to get all I needed to know from Dr. Rex.

A nurse took me into the room and waited for the doctor to come in. When Dr. Rex came into the room, he had a big smile on his face.

"Why the smile?" I asked.

"Well, it looks like I have a bit of good news" he said.

"Oh?"

"I got back the results from your blood test, and it looks like the rapid test results were wrong. It's what we call a false positive."

"Does that mean what I think it means?"

"Yes it does."

I was in tears. "Really?" I managed to say.

"Yes."

Once I had my breathing under control and wiped all the water off my face I said, "How is that possible?"

He began to explain. "Well, it's like this. Among 1,000 people who do not have disease, rapid tests will be falsely positive in zero to nine people, depending on the test. This is the main reason for not relying on a single positive test for diagnosis. As we discussed last time, all positive initial tests must be confirmed with a Western blot. When both tests are positive, the likelihood of a person being HIV infected is greater than 99 percent."

"Oh, my God," I stammered.

"Yeah. It doesn't happen often, but you were a lucky one."

"I was."

"Well Roberto, I think you are a bright kid. Sorry ... a bright 'young man' who has a bright future ahead. Please be more careful next time you have sexual intercourse. I know that it can be hard to stop when you are in the heat of the moment to grab a condom, but better safe than sorry."

"I promise I will. I'll probably go without sex for a long while."

"Good, but don't go overboard now. I don't want you to completely stop. Don't go cold turkey because of a scare. Just be more careful. Nothing wrong with having a little fun every now and then."

"I understand. Thank you."

"Do you have anymore questions?"

"No sir." I was relieved to be done.

William tried and tried to call me every other day, but I never answered. I just couldn't deal with him and his crazy boyfriend. It was too much drama and not something I wanted to get into again. Eventually, William got the message, and he gave up trying to make contact with me. After this close call, I swore to myself that I would never be this stupid or careless again.

Chapter Seven:

Focus

The best thing about this line of work they call modeling was that I had enough money to leave the hellhole of the place I was living. Not to brag of anything, but I was actually named the highest paid male model of the year. Crazy, right? I saved every penny I earned and was very careful of how I spent my money. I needed and desperately wanted a change. Even though I was away a lot due to work, living with Shaun was extremely stressful, and I could not handle being around his downer attitude. I had been living in that apartment for close to two years, and I was ready to move. I started looking for apartments everywhere, but specifically in the West Hollywood and Westwood areas; anything from one-bedrooms to studios … and I looked everywhere: newspapers, online ads, and even driving around the neighborhoods to see if there were any for rent that weren't posted online.

And I kept coming up with nothing. Everything I saw was ugly or crazy overpriced. None of them felt right.

I found this tiny shoebox of a condo in the middle of West Hollywood by accident. It was located on top of a small coffee shop where I had stopped by to get a cup of coffee. By chance, I looked up and saw a "for rent" sign in the window. I called the number on the sign, not expecting much. The man answered and told me he was upstairs if I wanted to take a peek at the place, and of course I went up to check it out.

The apartment was owned by this really sweet older gay gentleman named Ralph. He greeted me with a strong handshake on the side stairs of the building that went into the apartment. He was around 5'4" with grey hair, light brown eyes, bushy eyebrows, thin lips and a mole on his left cheek. He looked a bit like he could be Robert De Niro's older brother. He must have been in his late 70s, but that little guy sure moved around fast.

"Well aren't you a handsome young grasshopper," he said.

"Thank you, sir."

"Okay, you are actually the first person to take a look at the place, and I hope you'll be the last. I'm too old to go through this craziness and too cheap to hire a real estate guy."

"Okay."

"How old are you again?"

"22 years old."

"Oh okay. Kind of young, but if you have the money, why not? I can tell you are responsible. You're an old soul, aren't you?"

"Yes sir, I am."

"The eyes give it away."

"Oh. Okay." It made me giggle a bit.

"Well, back to business. The place isn't big or anything fancy. It's a 345-square-foot apartment with high ceilings, a divider wall that divides the living room from the bedroom, with one small bathroom that has a tub and shower head, two oversized windows that give you a nice little view of downtown and great sunlight all day. It comes with air conditioning and a heater; it has a nice but small and workable kitchen, hardwood floors, a big closet located in the living room and a small space for the bedroom area where a queen sized bed fits next to drawers built into the wall. This place is perfect for a young bachelor like yourself. All I'm asking for is $900 every month. I guarantee you won't find any other place cheaper around here."

I looked around at every corner of the apartment,

thinking it over. I was about to say yes when Ralph said, "This was the apartment I shared with my late departed partner of 26 years. This was our love nest where we took care of each other. I have a lot of great memories here, but since he's been gone, this isn't a place I want to be. Not without him. Maybe this apartment will bring you happiness, too."

"Thank you for sharing you story, and it's actually perfect for me. I'll take it."

"It's yours, kid."

I couldn't pack my things fast enough after I signed the lease to my small studio apartment. Shaun seemed so sad to see me go, and how could he not be? His company and only "friend" was leaving, and he would be alone for who knows how long. I prayed for whoever else moved into that apartment, because they'd need it. He helped me pack my things all while trying to convince me to stay, telling me that I should rethink this and that I was going to miss him. I wasn't going to be mean or anything, so I simply gave him a hug, told him thank you for everything, and out the door I went.

Now with a new place to live and a steady job that was pretty flexible, I decided to head back to school and finish my bachelor's degree in English. After all, I only had a few credits left to complete, and it was about time I got it done. I enrolled at UCLA (University of California, Los Angeles) for these three classes that I needed. I was excited to be in this atmosphere again and improve my writing skills, sharpen my analytic abilities, and broaden my literary knowledge. What hurt the most was that the fees were ridiculous. No wonder most people in America are struggling to find money for higher education. I was thankful to have the funds.

My very first class was "American Fiction to 1900," which was an early morning class. I wasn't too excited about that, but somehow I made it on time. In fact, I was so early that there was only two other people in the room. An awkward, geeky Chinese girl with glasses whose name might be Koko (it was stickered on the back of her laptop) was up in front right in the middle of the classroom. She had her nose in the class textbook getting some pre-reading done. The second person was a guy wearing a hoodie, hiding in the back of the room. I couldn't see his face because he looked like he was sleeping. I sat myself in the middle row on the right side of the room to keep an eye on both, because I was sure they'd be my competition for the highest grade in the class.

The class started and only a few more people showed up. Everyone in the class had at least one empty seat next to them on both sides, which meant that everyone kept to themselves. It was kind of funny seeing people being willingly anti-social. I looked back at the hoodie guy, and his head was still down on the table resting on his hands, but from what I could tell, he was awake and paying attention, just with his face covered by his hood. Maybe he had a fun night?

I wasn't sure if he always partied the night before or what, but he kept doing the same thing. He would wear mostly hoodies, and when he wasn't, he'd have a hat on that would always cover his face. At first, I was very curious about hoodie guy, but after a while, I stopped caring to the point that I forgot about him.

One day after being told by our professor that our next big exam would be at the end of the week and would count for 60 percent of our grade, I was stopped in the hallway by hoodie guy.

"Roberto, got a minute?" he asked.

"Oh, hey. Yeah?" I still couldn't see his face.

"Would you be interested in having a studying session with me? I could use some help getting ready for this test."

"Oh. With me?"

"Yeah, you seem to know your stuff."

"Thanks. Sure … would be fun to go over things with someone else. What's your name, by the way?" I asked. Maybe I could finally call him something other than "hoodie guy."

"Marco. So, when is a good time for you to meet up?"

"Nights this week are pretty open for me."

"Does tonight work?" I still couldn't see his face. Only his lips were moving and visible.

"Yeah."

While he wrote down information on a paper, he said, "Let's meet at my place. Do you drive? Or need to be picked up?"

"I drive."

He handed me the piece of paper and said, "Cool. Meet me at 8:00? Here is my address."

"Okay."

"See you there."

Right when I was going to ask him why he keeps his face hidden, he quickly walked away. I just kept thinking, "what an odd ball."

At exactly 8:00 pm, I went to the address which was in Beverly Hills. The home looked like it was cut out of an architecture magazine. It was hidden by a moss-covered brick wall and two big jacaranda trees with really pretty purple flowers, and from what I could see, it was a two-story Mediterranean-influenced design with a contemporary style … definitely modern. His parents must be super rich.

I rang the doorbell and his voice came on the intercom, "Hey come in." I heard the buzzer and entered.

I knocked on the door and Marco Ellis Ward, the famous young 20-year-old Hollywood heartthrob, was there to greet me.

"Are you my studying buddy?" I managed to

ask.

"Yeah. Don't you remember?"

"Bitch, I never actually saw your face. You kept hiding it behind hoodies and hats. I guess now I know why!"

"Oh … right. Sorry."

"Okay. Well, nice to officially meet you, Marco. Ready to study?"

He smiled and said, "Yeah!"

Chapter Eight:

Secret

So there I was, sitting in a really comfortable modern Monaco black leather sectional sofa with my study partner … the "hoodie guy," who happened to be none other than movie star Marco Ellis Ward. I was trying so hard not be nervous, but how could I not be? This study session at his house threw me for a loop, and I hate to admit it, but I had a small crush on Marco; well, as far as liking what I saw on the movies and magazines.

Marco came from an acting family and had been a professional actor since he was a toddler. America saw him grow up right before our eyes. He went from a cute and sensitive kid in daytime television, to a bad-boy teenager in award-winning Indie films, to a young and hunky Hollywood heartthrob. He was 5'8" tall, with dark brown curly hair, brownish-green eyes and a perfectly sculpted and muscular body – everyone's dream man.

"So, should we get started?" he asked.

"Yeah," I answered.

"Would you like something to drink or snack on before we start?"

"Water please."

"Coming up."

I was trying hard not to let him know that he was making me nervous. I didn't want to freak out this handsome straight man or to make him feel uncomfortable. After he handed me the water, I gathered my confidence and focused my energy. We opened our textbooks and went over every piece of material we had gone over in class and everything that might possibly be on the test. I quizzed him and went over everything a couple of times until it felt second nature to both of us.

"Well, I think you, sir, are more than ready for this test, and so am I," I told him as I closed my textbook.

"I do feel ready," he said smiling. I was packing up my things when he added, "Oh, just leave it. Dinner is ready in the kitchen."

"Dinner?" I asked, as he began to stand up.

"Yeah. My chef just cooked us up a little something. I figured we'd be hungry after we finished."

"I am a little hungry."

"Good. Follow me." I followed him into the kitchen, which was as big as my whole apartment. The walls, cabinets and drawers were all painted blood red and black. In the middle of the room the long wooden dining table was set for two. The chef in the kitchen elegantly served us both a plate of gourmet turkey burgers, then discretely went back to his kitchen duties.

"Burgers okay?" my friend asked.

"I'm a vegetarian."

"Oh. Sorry! Chef Josh can whip up anything you want."

"I'm just kidding. I'm not vegetarian, and the burger looks good. Thank you."

He had a good laugh.

We talked about his love of his job, the many failed relationships he'd had, and the fact that everyone including his family didn't really support him going back to school, but to him it was important to finish. I told him that I related, and that I respected him for doing what he wanted. At first he comes off as a quiet man, but once you get to know him, he's quite outgoing, interesting and hilarious! But what I really liked about him was how much he values his family and his love of

God. Then he started asking me questions:

"So, do you have a girlfriend?"

"No girlfriend."

"I have a nice friend who you might like. She's cool and down to earth."

"No thanks. I'm actually gay."

"Oh."

The "big reveal" felt a little weird, so I tried to warm things up. "Yeah … no loose bacon strips from me, I'm more of a sausage kind of guy."

He laughed hard, "I like that!"

"Well, I'm glad you do." I looked at my watch and couldn't believe the time. "Wow, it's getting close to 2:00 am. I should be heading home now."

"You don't have to. You can stay at one of the guest rooms if you want. That's what they are there for."

"That's sweet of you to offer. It really is, but I prefer sleeping in my own bed." As we walked back to the living room, I noticed that someone had put all my papers, notebooks, and my textbook back in my bag for me.

"Who cleaned up?" I asked.

"The maid."

"Well, that was easy. Tell her thank you for me."

"I will." We made our way to the door, and I started to say my goodbyes. "Well I had a great time studying and hanging out."

"Same here, man."

"Nice to finally crack the mystery of the 'hoodie man.'"

"I know, it's a little weird isn't it?"

"A bit … but it's understandable. People are crazy out there, and safety first."

"Yeah …"

"So, why did you trust me enough to reveal yourself to me? I mean, I could have potentially been one of those crazy people."

"Not sure. Something just told me that I could trust you."

"Oh … okay. Well, goodnight and thanks again for dinner."

"Good night."

He leans over and opens his arms for a hug, and we embraced. That just might have been the best hug I had ever gotten. It felt nice, warm, and a chill went through me, feeling his muscled body so close to mine. This hug was a little long, or maybe it was just in my head and it was quicker than I imagined, but my mind told me it was longer. We let go, I got in my car, and I went home.

After that night, we became quick friends, and both killed our test we had studied for with a nearly perfect score! I even ended up moving seats next to him, which was his idea, not mine. The final day of school was around the corner, and as we got closer to that date, Marco and I become even closer. How much closer could I get with a straight Hollywood movie star, I thought?

One extremely warm Saturday afternoon, he called me up to tell me that he was bored and asked if I wanted to come over for a swim. I was in a desperate need of a good cool down, and I told him I would be right over. When I got there, he was shirtless and just wearing board shorts that hung pretty low on his V line. I was embarrassed because I could tell he caught me looking at his body.

"Sorry," I muttered.

"Don't be. I work hard. Actually, it would be kind of an insult if you didn't look! I'm just messing with you. It's all good."

He laughed and gave me a hug. Marco had a way of making you feel comfortable even in awkward situations. How can someone be this cool? We headed to his back yard where the pool was located. For some reason, I thought there would be other people invited to take a dip in the pool, but it was just me. He went over and laid in one of the lounge chairs that were near the pool. He handed me a towel and I placed it along with my bag in the chair next to him. I took off my muscle shirt and dove into the pool. As I was taking a few laps around the pool, I noticed him staring at me every time I would take a breath of air. Again, maybe it was just in my mind, but I couldn't shake off the feeling. I got out of the pool and lay in the chair.

"You are a pretty good swimmer," he told me.

I looked over to him, smiled, and asked, "Do you think so? Thanks man, it felt good to take some laps."

"Well, thank you for the company and saving

me from complete boredom."

After baking in the sun for a while, we went over to a small table near the house with a big umbrella. There was so much to choose from: bottled water, a jug of strawberry lemonade, sandwiches, mini-burgers, and all kinds of fruit. We continued talking about everything – his upcoming movies, my modeling and our families. It felt good to talk to him. Hours literally flew by when I was around him. Suddenly, the sun was already going down, and it was time for me to go.

"Well, I should get going, Marco."

"Oh, okay." I went over and as I was grabbing my things from the chair he said, "Why don't you shower here and that way you don't drive back with that chlorine water on your skin."

"Oh, sure." I didn't think much of it and he led me to the big bathroom where the shower was.

"Here you go. Shampoos are on the wall and fresh towels are next to the door," he said.

"Thank you." He stepped out of the bathroom, and I got in the shower. I started to wash my body off, and halfway through the shower, a thought occurred: I didn't bring any extra clothes to change into. I supposed I'd just wear the same clothes I came in. I turned off the water and stepped out to dry myself. I looked towards the door and saw Marco just frozen, still holding clothes for me. He was just starring at my naked body, and I noticed a boner through his bathing suit. I could tell he was embarrassed, but wasn't looking away.

"Is that for me?"

"Yeah … I figured you could use some clothes."

"I wasn't talking about the clothes." He dropped the clothes on the floor, and I dropped the towel.

I headed straight for him and we started to kiss, hard and passionately, all while my hands gripped his perfectly muscled ass. God, he had great lips, and he knew exactly how to use them. I hate to say this, but I felt like one of his sexy girlfriends in one of his movies. In a matter of seconds, we ended up in the bedroom next door, both of our naked bodies rubbing against each other on the bed. We went from kissing lips, to licking nipples, to jerking our tools. As soon as the lube and the condoms came out, I knew this was going to go all the way.

All while still kissing Marco, I started to get mentally prepared because something in me told me that I was going to have to bottom. I pumped myself up, told myself that it'd be okay, that I just had to relax, take my time, and breathe a lot. I pumped myself up so much that I was actually looking forward to giving over myself to him. He gave me one final kiss, turned around face down on the bed and showed off all his back muscles, and when he hoisted his ass in the air, I noticed a cute mole on his left cheek. He then handed me the lube followed by a condom.

"I have never done this before, but … I want you in me," he whispered.

Even though I was a bit disappointed that he wanted to bottom, I couldn't get the lube and condom on fast enough. I took my time getting him relaxed, and then he was ready for me to go in. I started slow and then picked up speed. I kept asking if he was okay and if he was enjoying himself. He didn't talk much, but he moaned super loud, telling me he was having fun, and I was doing my job right. We went at it for close to three hours.

After the dirty was done, it wasn't weird at all. He acted

normal, told me that he had fun and couldn't wait to do it again. As I was about to leave his house, he kissed me, told me he'd see me in class, and that to please keep this between us. I agreed.

Our friendship was the same after that, but maybe a bit better being secret lovers and all. It wasn't perfect, but it was sure steamy. He had this weird and kinky thing that turned him on so much. Not sure if I would call it a fetish, but it was something I'd never heard of before. It was sort of an abs fetish, but what we did with them was strange … but I went along with it. He liked abs on abs, but here is the weird part: he blew out his stomach and I sucked in my stomach and then we switched back and forth. It was this push and pull effect. For some reason, doing it made him cream so quickly. He enjoyed and preferred this more than actual intercourse.

Marco had so much trust in me that he eventually started taking me to small and super-secret Hollywood Hills parties. These were the kind of parties where you have to be personally invited to, sign a confidentiality paper, and even turn in all cell phones at the door. These were also for gay men only. The people attending these parties were Hollywood actors, directors, singers and even some well-known athletes. It did freak me out how many of the people I thought were straight weren't at all. Some, if not most of the people in the room, had girlfriends and wives in their public lives, but I guess they also had separate lives where they would secretly have their sex with men. At first it was a fun experience seeing these famous people be themselves, listening to the fun music, eating delicious food, and peeking in on and sometimes participating in the sex rooms. My opinion quickly changed when he asked me to work for him.

Photographers had taken pictures of us having lunch and coming out of parties that the magazines posted those pictures with titled, "Is Marco Ellis Ward dating this male supermodel?" His solution was to ask me to be his really well paid "assistant" and still have a down low relationship.

I couldn't do that. I had my own thing going for me, and frankly, I deserved better. I wanted to live my life as a proud gay man, so I refused to get back in my closet. I just had to say goodbye to Marco as a lover and hang out a little less because I was starting to get true feelings for him. I knew I could never be his man the way I wanted it.

I felt bad for him because he was stuck in this place and would probably be there for a while. All his "people" controlled his life and didn't let him come out as a gay man because they were scared that if he did, he wouldn't bring in those multi-million dollar movie deals anymore, meaning they'd be out of a job.

I told Marco we should just be friends and not sleep together again. Sex with friends complicates things, and I didn't want to have my heart broken in the end. He cried, and I cried, but he understood. We remained friends and at the end of the final day of class, we gave each other a big hug. He went off to film a movie in Canada, and I went to New York for a few weeks to work a bit. Even though things didn't work out with Marco the way I wanted, in the end, I still had a good friend and was proud that I managed to finish my bachelor's degree in English!

Chapter Nine:

The Agent

When I first met a rich real-estate guy for the Hollywood stars, I wasn't really impressed. His name was Ethan, and honestly, I didn't think twice about him. He had come over to deliver a DVD that my good photographer friend had borrowed from me. It was 7:00 am, and I was only half-awake when I received his text message. He said that he was close by and was going to drive through to drop off my movie. He drove in with his titanium-colored Range Rover. Although I figured he was pushing 50, he looked older. He was balding on the top of his head, wore a plain gray T-shirt, ripped, but very expensive jeans and topped it all off with dumpy old man loafers. What was going on with his fashion sense …who dressed this guy?

"Hello, Ethan here," he said as he held up my DVD.

I smiled, leaned in to get my DVD and just said, "Hi, Roberto." As I started to walk back to my door, he started making conversation.

"So, you are the famous Roberto." I looked at him with a weird, surprised look.

"Famous?" I asked.

"Yeah, I saw your pictures. Kind of a fan," he said with a big smile.

What was this guy's deal? I thought he was just dropping off my movie, and he was actually hitting on me.

"Well thank you," I managed.

"You're welcome. We should go hang out sometime. I hear you are very active. Maybe go for a hike sometime?"

I thought about saying no, but to be honest I kind of felt sorry for him. He looked like he needed a friend or for someone to finally say yes to him. I figured why not and we did. Every other day, we would go hiking together at Runyon Canyon and just talk. Well, he actually did most of the talking and I just listened. Like most power gays in this town, he talked about everything, from all his famous "friends" and clients to where he's been in the world. I didn't really think much about it. I figured he was just trying hard to woo me or get in my pants. At first I just saw him as a goofy friend … my outdoor activities buddy. I didn't care who he knew, how much money he had in the bank or anything like that. I treated him no differently than anyone else.

But after weeks of hanging out as friends, he asked me if we can try really dating each other. I figured, why not? I was open-minded. Sure, he was much older, had absolutely no fashion sense, and kind of on the odd side but he also had his good traits. He treated me right, respected me, and I truly enjoyed his company.

He had a wonderful home in the heart of West Hollywood and a second in the very warm Palm Springs. Both, of course, included a pool and a sauna. He was really into doing something different every night: a party here and a movie there.

But what he really loved were surprises. A trip to San Francisco on a private jet was definitely a surprise. His birthday came around, and all his friends were having this huge dinner party in his honor. He was turning the big 5-0. We ran around all day doing errands, we did some shopping, washed the car, took the dog out for a walk, swam in the pool (naked of course) and then headed to the hot sauna to relax.

It was getting around the time to leave for the party, but he didn't want to leave yet. He wanted to kiss some more and just hang out naked.

"You are the only person that I want to be with today. I don't care about the stupid party," he told me. We rode his motorcycle to the party in Hollywood Hills, and of course we were late to his own party. He introduced me to all his friends as his "extremely handsome boyfriend." It was a good crowd. By "good" I mean they were nice and chatty, not bitchy and judgmental. They all seemed to be interested in what I had to say and went out of their way to make me feel welcomed. The group consisted of all kinds of people. There were gay and straight directors, well- known photographers, actresses, actors, painters, and even two drag queens. He always kept me close by, holding my hand at all times and asking me if I was okay or having fun every ten minutes. It was a good feeling.

Even though Ethan and I got along fine, and he was a great kisser, I started to notice something that I didn't before: we were never really physical toward each other. Sure, we had fooled around here and there. I mean, we slept together naked in bed, swam in the pool naked, showered together, and hung out in the sauna naked but we never actually had sex. I knew that he was a strict top because he had to be in "control," and I was fine with that. Every time I felt like it was going to happen – the lube was out, he was eating me out – all of the sudden it just wouldn't happen. He had this huge, beautiful 10-inch cut dick, and the problem was that he couldn't or wouldn't get fully erect for me. I felt bad at first. Was I not attractive enough? Was I doing something wrong? When I finally had the awkward conversation with him, he told me it was because, according to him, I "intimidated him." That made things difficult. He refused to bottom, and he wasn't able to perform. So that didn't give us a lot of options. I tried to stay positive, telling him that sex didn't matter so much and that things will get better and eventually fix themselves. But they didn't.

The relationship got to the point where it wasn't working out at all. I was to the point where I was fed up. Not only was I extremely sexually frustrated, but he started to act differently towards me as well. He started to be too obsessive and acted like he owned me. He had to know where I was and who I was with at all time. He never trusted me, not even when I was with my family. He felt like I was too good for him and didn't understand why I was with him. He constantly thought that I was "cheating" on him with the Starbucks guy, or the mailman, or my best friend, or even my lesbian friend. In my limited experience, I already knew that often, rich men act childish and immature but I had hoped Ethan was different. I was wrong.

I could not handle these ridiculous insecurities. He was rude to waiters, valet people, and every retail staff member he came into contact with. He always talked down to them. I started noticing it more and more. His cocaine habit was getting out of hand, too. I think that's what made him flip into crazy ugly personalities. I hated that he did drugs … absolutely hated it. I never did any of the drugs, but who was I to tell him to stop? It finally got to the point where he was constantly trying to put me down, commenting on things like my job, my looks, where I came from, and even my uncircumcised penis. He would make weird jokes that were hurtful when we were alone or in front of other people. To him, he was more important or worth more than me, and it was as if I was just a pretty accessory to show off. I was no one's property. I knew I had to end it. So the next morning, I told him that we had to talk.

"Hey can we talk for a second?" I asked.

Barely looking up from his breakfast he grunted, "What's up? Make it quick."

"I'll make it quick and easy. Look Ethan, I don't think this is going to work."

"Huh?" The fork literally dropped out of his mouth in surprise.

"I think we want different things. I don't think I am what you are looking for and I don't think you are for me either."

"What do you mean?"

"Well in all honesty it's not really working out. It's not even just about the not having sex thing. It's not that important to me. It's your insecurities and the way you come off to me and towards other people. You come off as a dick."

"I do?"

"Yeah, you do."

"Lies."

"I have tried to tell you this many, many times. I can't be with someone who's … sorry for the use of the word, but … an Asshole." He stood there in silence, shocked at what I was telling him. "Plus, I don't think you really want a relationship. You just want someone to own. It's supposed to be 50-50, as equals, and you treat me like an assistant of yours. And, by the way, I know you have something going on the side. Does his girlfriend know that you been fucking around with her boyfriend?"

"What? How did you know?" I had broken the silence.

"It's a bit obvious. He's an unqualified assistant who constantly messes up the tiniest tasks. Sure he's handsome and all, but I thought it was odd that he automatically hated me the minute I walked in your front door. Why wouldn't he? Unless he thought I was taking his cash-cow away from him. Oh, and what really gave it away was when you lent me your desktop computer to check my email. You left a movie clip opened up on your screen of you having a threesome with him and another girl, and there was also a picture of him cleaning your pool naked. Who does that?"

"Oh … well it's just a bit of fun. He likes to clean the pool naked. It doesn't mean a thing. I'm a man, I can't control myself. It's just sex. I don't love him. I love you."

"Just sex? Do you know how messed up that sounds? I realize that people with money seem to think they can just do anything they please; that rules don't apply to them. Everything is a joke and they don't take anything seriously, except for work."

"I know I can be childish at times but —"

"If I'm going to give my heart to someone, I expect them to be faithful. To only be mine. I'm very old fashioned. You knew that." He walked away from the kitchen and toward the bed where he took a seat right next to me. He began to cry to himself without making any noise, just tears coming down his cheeks.

I didn't let myself get affected by his emotion. "Sorry. I just can't do this anymore. I had fun, and you really aren't a terrible guy, but this is just not a good fit. I'm not what you want, and you aren't what I'm looking for. I do have love for you. I do. If it was some other guy in this town, they might pretend that everything is fine and see how much they can get from you. I'm not like that. I love you enough to let you go. We shouldn't be wasting each other's time on something that isn't right." I kissed him on his forehead and walked away.

After that day he, of course, told all of our mutual friends that he broke up with me. He said that I was cheating on him and that I treated him like shit, which was absolute bullshit. Then, like a hurt little kid, he started sending me nasty text messages to try and make me feel bad and so he could feel better about himself.

He sent messages like "I can't believe you broke up with me. I was the best thing that will ever happen to you. It was a big mistake letting me go. You are stupid. You aren't as hot as you think you are."

I was being polite and tried to be bigger person. But after the beating I had been taking for days, I'd finally had enough. I was tired of being the nice guy. So, I took a screen shot of the conversation and posted it online. All of our friends saw it and saw his true colors. I guess he didn't think of that when he sent me all of those messages. I ended up blocking him from contacting me online and changed my number. Boy, was I glad that mess was over.

Chapter Ten:

James

I was at my gym early in the morning for a full-body intense work out. It was so early in fact, that it was still dark outside. Only a handful of intrepid people working out at this crazy hour. My gym (AKA: gay church) was the biggest gay gym in the Los Angeles area. I was in the zone with headphones in both ears. When I work out, I go into my own little world; other people don't exist. I'm focused on what I'm doing and try not to have conversations with people.

Most other people use the gym time to socialize. Not me. I was working out my chest, arms, and back that morning. It had been a few days since I had a good work out because getting things situated in the new apartment took lots of time, and I was still trying to get acclimated to the neighborhood.

So there I was, killing myself on my work out, feeling super out-of-shape and disgusting with sweat running down my whole body. When I took a second to drink some water, I felt a tap on my shoulder. A Ron Jeremy-looking guy in his late 60s – overweight, balding and with some serious body odor – was standing freakishly close to me and signaled to me to take off my headphones. I reluctantly complied.

"Hey, handsome. I haven't seen you around here. What's your name?" he asked.

A bit irritated, I replied, "Roberto. Sorry but I have to really finish this work out. I'm in a hurry. Can I help you man?"

"Um … yeah … mind if I work out with you R-r-r-r-r-roberto?"

Hearing him try rolling the R's while saying my name made me feel very creeped out. The way he was looking me up and down made me feel like he was raping me with his eyes. Trying to not be a dick, I politely responded, "Oh, I only have to finish one more set."

He presses even closer … so close that I thought he was going to kiss me. As he moves forward, I moved back.

"What? You think you are too hot for me or too good to share the machine?" he blurted out. I almost lost my temper and smacked the man. The polite etiquette at the gym for this situation is to have him wait his turn. I only had one more to go. If he had waited three minutes, he would have the machine by now, but instead he's being dramatic. I wasn't scared. I could easily take him if things got violent. I was just a bit annoyed at the whole situation.

"Why don't you give me a little kiss? I bet you'll like it."

He was about to walk forward again when a hand grabs him from the shoulder and stops him saying, "Leave him alone, for fuck's sake."

The pervert said, "Who's going to stop me?" as he started to turn around. I looked to get a better view of the other guy. I was instantly attracted. He was in his early 40's but extremely handsome. He was around 6'4" with misty, gray-colored eyes; he was built like a Greek god. Even his muscles had muscles … a big chest, big arms and big butt.

"I am. If I have to," he said calmly. He had a sexy and rough accent that sounded very European. With one look at this big guy, the pervert ran away like his sagging butt was on fire.

"Thanks man, but I could have taken care of myself. I'm a big boy," I said, maybe a bit too defensively.

"I'm sure of it, but I couldn't help myself from giving you a hand," he said as he locked eyes with me.

"Well, I appreciate your help in any case. Very sweet of you mister …"

"My name is James. And anytime," he said, flashing me a smile. He had a big, firm handshake.

"Roberto. Nice to meet you."

"Same here. Well, I'll let you work out."

James slowly headed back towards his own workout area. Just as I'm thinking how weird this all was, getting hit on by a disgusting perv, then rescued by a hunk, James stops, quizzically put a hand to his head, tugs at his hair and turns back around. He looked at me but seemed at a loss for what to say.

I smiled, raised an eyebrow, and said, "Yeah?"

"Hey, I know this is a bit awkward, seeing as there was just a creep hitting on you. I never do this, but again, I can't help myself but to ask you. Would you maybe be interested in grabbing some coffee sometime?"

" Wait," I stopped him. "Was the other guy working for you and this is was your plan all along?"

"No! No. I swear."

131

I laughed and said, "I'm just kidding. Sure, I'll grab coffee with you."

After exchanging information, I concentrated enough to finish a really great workout even with him constantly on my mind.

For my first "date" with James, we decided to meet at a small local coffee shop. It was one of those hole-in-the-wall places owned by an elderly gay couple. I loved this place, especially since it wasn't one of those trendy "to be seen" places.

Art by local artists decorated the walls. A piano anchored the rear section, and a whole second level had couches and chairs for sitting. As usual, I was super early, so I went ahead and ordered coffee. Upstairs, strategically seated with a good view of the front door, I waited for him to arrive.

When James finally spotted me, it seemed his whole face lit up with happiness. He ordered an iced coffee and bounded up the stairs, two at a time, and yet never spilled a drop from his open-topped mug. Before even saying hello he gave me a big hug. I loved the feeling of his muscled body pressed against mine.

"Am I late? Have you been waiting long?" he asked.

"No. Not at all," I quickly replied.

He was not only a very handsome 42-year-old engineer, but he was a sweetheart, too. What I was most surprised about was his honesty. He was very open about everything … and I mean everything.

He talked about being born in Australia and how he enjoyed living in the United Kingdom for 8 years. He had been married once at a very young age, but he felt he was forced into it by his family. He had two children: a 16 year-old boy and a 20 year-old girl, and that both – along with his ex-wife – were understanding when he finally came out to them. They wanted him to live his life the way he was meant to. They stayed back in London and truly hoped he would find the man of his dreams. Now, hearing all this information would scare off many gay guys. In the least, they would most-likely be put off by all his "baggage."

But I didn't care. It just didn't matter to me. I was really into him, and not just because his accent was dreamy. He was a real man and knew who he was. I wasn't one of those 20 year-olds only thinking of partying and getting high. I had always been an old soul anyway. I felt we were both on the same wavelength, and the attraction was off the charts! I wanted this man.

After a good two-and-a-half hours of talking, we were being kicked out by management because they were closing. The night ended like a scene from a Hollywood movie: he kissed me into ecstasy before I reluctantly had to end the night and head back home. He had such sweet and soft lips against mine.

I was in heaven just from that kiss, but when we had sex for the first time he raised the bar of perfection ten notches. How so? Let's just say he could rock the nicknames "baby arm" and "bootylicious."

We began texting each other at all hours, day or night. They were silly things at first, like how work was going, whether he pushed his muscles to the max at the gym that day, and what he ate for lunch. Then the texts turned to more serious things: what we wanted out of the future … our dreams and goals. It was a nice change from my ex, the real-estate dickhead. James was extremely charming, and I constantly felt like my whole body just needed to be next to him. After dating a month-and-a-half, James told me on one of our dates that his company transferred to another city. He only had one week to move to San Diego.

He was very sad when he told me the news, and said he didn't want me to live so far away. He was over-the-moon when I made the decision to move to San Diego with him. I knew it was a bit crazy, but I had to find out if he was "the one", and my job was super flexible anyway. I might be crazy hopeless for love, but I wasn't stupid. I was also keeping my apartment. I packed some of my things, told Ralph the building owner that I was going on vacation, and if he could keep an eye on it for me every now and then, I would appreciate it. Ralph had looked in on my place at different times when I had traveled overseas, as well. I paid him a year's worth of rent in advance and headed over to San Diego with James.

Our house was a cute, two-story building that had recently been refurbished. This was my new home. Time flew by, and after being together for 5 months, we were getting into a good routine together. We would cook healthy food, work out at the gym every night, have steady sex, and do fun outdoor stuff like camping. I would still fly to Los Angeles and New York to do photoshoots to make money and help with the bills. I was happy.

But the happiness didn't last long. Some relationships change like a light switch turned on and off. Ours was far more like slowly turning a dimmer switch farther and farther until the room is almost without light. Everything was starting to fall apart. He wasn't the same man I met five months ago. He became cold towards me and was very distant. He was lost in his thoughts a lot, and I didn't know what was wrong. I tried asking him about it but he would just brush it off and say things like, "Yeah everything is okay," or "Nothing to worry about. Just thinking." But I knew deep down something was up. What was the problem? I didn't want to have another failed relationship. I didn't think I could handle it. Maybe this was in my head and nothing was wrong.

When he came in from work one night, he went straight into the kitchen. He didn't kiss me or even said hello to me. Something was wrong and it was time we talked about it.

"Can we talk?" I asked him.

"Sure," he said

"You've been acting weird for a few days now. What's wrong?"

"Nothing."

"Stop. Please just tell me. Something is obviously wrong. You've been super distant. It's awkward."

"Sorry you feel that way," he whispered.

"So? What's going on? Talk to me. We can't fix this if you won't talk about it."

"There is nothing to fix."

"I'm not sure why you are acting this way but I can't stay here with a man who won't talk about his problems. We are supposed to be a team. Talk to me."

"You don't have to stay then."

Stop, hold the press! Did he just say that? A great and once-passionate relationship just dies with six words spoken without emotion?

"Fine. If that's how you want it, I'll go."

The next day, I had packed my stuff and I was all ready to go. I got a rental truck, and James (who was now shirtless) started to help me place things inside the truck, not saying a word or even looking at me. When I placed the last box in the truck, James was next to the moving truck waiting for me.

"So this is goodbye," I told him.

"Yeah … I'm sorry."

"I still don't know what the hell happened but okay." He looked down but didn't say anything. "Well, it was nice while it lasted. I want to wish you the best of luck, but next time, try and talk about what's in your head. "

"Again. I'm sorry," he managed.

Trying not to be bitter, I hugged him and wished him well. I got in the truck and drove off, tears running down my face. The last thing I wanted was to be alone with my thoughts, so I pushed the first pre-set station. As if on cue came the strumming of a guitar, followed by John Denver singing: "This is what it's like, falling out of love. This is the way you lose your very best friend. This is how it feels when it's all over. This is just the way true love ends."

Crazy coincidence like this you just can't make up.

Chapter Eleven:

Surprise, Surprise

I was out and about in a Santa Monica outdoor shopping mall just killing time and looking for a birthday present for my sister, but after hours of not finding the right gift, I was so tired that I took a break on a nearby bench and gazed at the rich carnival of life unfolding all around me.

It was fun just watching all the tourists with their cameras, taking pictures of everything in front of them. Suddenly, it was like the ocean of people parted. There he was, right in front of me.

I spotted Hunter (the ex boyfriend and love of my life from Washington state) inside the clothing store right across the bench I was sitting on. I panicked and I didn't know what to do. Was I seeing things? Maybe, but he wasn't going away. He was real, and there he was looking as good as ever. I did the only thing that made sense at that moment.

I ran.

I slipped into the restroom next to the store, took the closest stall, pulled down my shorts and pretended to go to the bathroom. I waited … and waited and waited, until I finally figured enough time had passed to venture back outside. I went to the sink and splashed water on my face. After I pulled myself together, I went to the door, put my sunglasses on, took a big breath and headed out.

You know how your mother always says tie your shoe laces, because if you leave them untied, you will trip and fall? Well I guess she was right.

I tripped on my shoelace as I walked out the door. But as I was falling, I extended both of my hands in front of me. When I landed, I turned my ridiculous-looking fall into a push up, just to make it seem like it was all on purpose. Unfortunately for my smooth move, my sunglasses tumbled off and my left hand landed on a sharp pebble, which hurt like a son-of-a-bitch.

"Are you alright?" said a voice in front of me.

"Yeah I'm fine. Thanks," I managed, shaking off the metaphorical dust and coming to my feet. I looked up in front of me, and there was this beautiful girl holding out her hand.

"Oh, thank you," I said, captivated by her beauty. She had green eyes, perfect white skin and rosy cheeks. Her long brown hair contrasted with her bright white shirt. With gold sandals and a bright gold belt accenting her form-fitting Daisy

Dukes, she looked fabulous. If she wasn't a model, she should have been.

She helped me get up and said to me, "Nice save with the fake push up." I instantly liked her.

"Ha! Thank you. I tried to play it cool."

"I'm Dawn."

"Roberto."

As soon as I said my name, a voice from behind came into the small hallway we were in and said, "Dawn, is everything okay?" I looked over and there he was: the love of my life. Hunter.

"Yeah, everything is fine. Hunter, this is Roberto," she said. I looked into his beautiful eyes, and I was taken back to Washington. All those emotions hit me like a wall of bricks.

"Roberto?" he stammered, sounding as shocked as I was. I felt like I was about to cry. I didn't want him to see me crying. I wanted to get out of there. I started to walk away. I looked at Dawn, and she had a confused look on her face, and as I walked past Hunter, he took my hand and stopped me.

"Wait a minute. Can we please talk? Please. I'm begging."

I wanted to say, "No. Get the hell away from me. You broke my heart. You left me waiting in Washington for you. Go to Hell." But instead … I don't know why … but what came out of my mouth was, "Okay."

He looked at Dawn and said, "I'll catch up with you later."

"How will you get home?" she asked.

"I'll be okay," he replied.

"Okay, babe. Nice meeting you Roberto."

We walked towards the beach and ended up at the end of the pier. I watched the ocean waves crash against the pylons, the seagulls flying above us, the families enjoying a day of perfect sunshine, and older people contentedly fishing, and I felt the warm sun on my back and fresh cool air on my face. We were just making small talk, but I figured I should be the first to start off a more-substantive conversation. Plus, I was curious about Dawn.

"So is she your girlfriend?"

He laughed and said, "Dawn? No. She is just my friend …er, roommate actually. She's kind of a big fruit fly."

"What's a fruit fly?" I asked.

"You know … a hag."

"Oh!" I exclaimed, and then burst into a fit of laughter. The offhand comment caught me by surprise and helped lighten the mood between us.

He paused for a second and then spoke: "Roberto. I want to say that I'm sorry. What I did was horrible, and I'd hate me if I were you. You probably even want to hit me right about now. But please, let me get all of this out." I didn't know what to say to him, so I just stayed quiet while he continued talking.

He continued: "I felt like I died after I did that to you. Like a zombie. I love you so much. So much. I never thought it would happen. It was a tough time for me. Here I was, madly in love with a guy, and I was in conflict with my beliefs. My religion really screwed me up. I even tried going into one of those 'clinics.' You know, the ones that supposedly help 'de-gay' you. That alone was a big issue. It took me out of the closet, and all my family found out … and my church, too. They did terrible things to me in that clinic. Unthinkable things. I ended up more confused, not knowing what was right and what was wrong."

"A few days after I left the clinic, I realized that love is all that matters in this world. By then it was too late. I went to Sheldon's house to see you, but you had already moved. He was furious at me and almost kicked my ass. He wouldn't tell me where you had gone, only that you had changed your number. I had no way to find you."

"You came looking for me?" I asked, astonished.

"Yes. I waited outside your house for days. I figured he was lying to me and you'd eventually come out … but you never did."

"Why are you here now?" I asked him.

"Sheldon watched me outside his street for weeks. One day, he came out to my car and told me to go home. I wouldn't. I suppose he took pity on me because he finally told me that you had moved to LA, but he wouldn't tell me your exact address. He said that if it was meant to be, that it would happen."

"So you moved here looking for me?" surprised.

"Yes. I packed my things, and I've been here ever since, waiting … and hoping you'd show up somewhere. Los

Angeles is a huge place … but I can't believe it. Here you are. Please forgive me. Please. I love you, Roberto."

He had such a sad face. Tears streamed down his cheeks so fast that wiping them away made no difference. His suffering hit my heart like a hammer. My body tightened up, a sensation of having all the air in my lungs sucked out. Goose-bumps popped up all over my body. My knees were weak and felt as if they would fail any minute. Blood rushed to my face, making me dizzy. This feeling was like nothing I had experienced before. Then the words just came tumbling out of my mouth as if nothing could stop them.

"I love you, too."

His face brightened up. "Do you forgive me?"

"Yes. I actually did a long time ago. I couldn't keep anger in my heart. I couldn't hate you. I had to let go of that anger. I had to try to understand your position and move on. It's all in the past."

"Does that mean you don't want to give me another chance?"

"Honestly, I'm scared to."

"Please don't be. I will never do anything like that to you again. Never. You are the one for me. You always have been and always will be. I love you Roberto. I want to make you happy. I can't imagine not being with you. I want to grow old with you."

I looked into his eyes and said, "I feel the same way."

He walked towards me and grabbed my hand. He moved slowly and leaned in for a kiss … it was small and tender but full of more passion and energy than I had ever felt in a kiss before. What he did next changed my life.

Bending down on one knee and taking a tiny black box from his pocket, Hunter said, "Roberto – I have loved you since the first time I set my eyes on you. You make me want to be a better man. You make me feel like I can do anything, and I am happiest when I'm next to you. I have been looking for you for a long time. I've been carrying this ring in my pocket, hoping I'd run into you. Will you please do me the honor of being my husband? Will you marry me?"

This was so unexpected and incredibly romantic. We were in the middle of the pier with all these strangers looking at us, taking pictures.

I looked down at him and softly said, "Yes." People clapped and cheered.

Hunter got up and kissed me again.

Chapter Twelve:

Parents

My parents had been begging me to come visit them for a while. They had moved to Palm Springs, a desert town about a two-hour drive from Los Angeles. They said they were "okay with my gay lifestyle." I figured enough time had passed since I came out to them that it would have been fine to introduce them to the man in my life – my true partner. This could show them that my feelings were legitimate and not a phase.

After getting engaged to Hunter, I was happier than I had ever been in my life, and I thought it would be about time that I would introduce him to my parents. It wasn't really my idea, to be honest. Hunter wanted me to reach out to them, especially since we were going to get married soon. I was a bit worried about it, especially since it would be the first time that I would ever bring another gay person to my parents' house.

So bringing my fiancé was a huge deal. I wasn't sure how my parents would react to him, but they had known for a while that I was dating someone. Still, true acceptance was a bit of a gray area, and I was nervous as to how my dad would react.

Driving to their home, I figured it would be a good time to talk over a game plan.

I looked over to him and said, "Hunter, if my father begins to be rude to you, or either of my parent's starts acting really mean, let's just leave, okay? Don't even argue back."

"I'm sure it will be fine," he replied.

"Promise me," I insisted.

"I promise."

"If for some reason my dad starts getting physical, then let me handle it. Okay?"

"You are really scared, aren't you? Babe, if things get out of hand, then we will just leave. If he tries to put a hand on you ... then I'm sorry, but I will have to step in."

"Well, I just want you to be prepared for anything. If things are bad, let's just leave. I don't want to put up with their shit or have you go through that. Cool?"

"Sure. We'll bolt if things get bad."

The drive felt like a slow march to the gallows, but finally we arrived at my parents' house. At least that's what the GPS said. It was a simple, one-story house with a coat of bright white paint. There was no grass in the front yard, but it was peppered with a few cactuses. The house was dotted with blue-colored windows with white curtains, but what really caught my attention was the big front door that seemed to grow larger and larger as we got closer.

"This is nice. Should we ring the door bell now?" Hunter asked. I stood there frozen … nervous, and not knowing quite how to respond. But before Hunter was able to ring the bell, the door swung open, and my mother walked out.

"Hey pumpkin! Oh, how I have missed you!" She gave me a big hug as I walked in the door. "And you must be Hunter." She scanned him head to toe and said in a softer voice, "We've heard some nice things about you."

Hunter put out his hand and said, "Well thank you. It's a pleasure to finally meet you."

"I'm Rosa Salas, Roberto's mom."

"Hello Rosa, it's so nice to be here … thank you for welcoming us to your home."

"Such a sweet man! I'm glad Roberto has a friend like you. Oh, I'm sorry! Boyfriend. So handsome, too!" she doted on him, pinching his cheek and leaning forward to give him a big embrace. "We give hugs around here."

Just as my mother was hugging the life out of Hunter, my father came up. This was the moment I was waiting for. I had prayed relentlessly that my dad would be civil to him.

My father shook Hunter's hand and said in his best broken English, "Welcome. I'm Miguel Salas, Roberto's father." He definitely had a good poker face … his expression was emotionless, though his words were inviting enough.

"Nice to meet you, sir," Hunter responded.

"Make yourself at home."

"Thank you."

He pretended to be nice, but I would catch him giving him the stink-eye every now and then. My dad ended up going to his corner of the house and just ignoring us completely. For the most part, he just sat and watched television. I figured that was a step in the right direction. I'd take "fake nice and being ignored dad" over the mean and loud man that lurked underneath.

To be fair, the men in our family aren't exactly known to be big talkers. My mom, on the other hand, took over every conversation. She seemed happy and super interested in him, asking Hunter everything about his life.

"So Hunter, what do you do for a living?"

"I am lawyer for a small law firm," Hunter responded.

"What a great job to have. Handsome and smart. You did well, Roberto," she said.

"I did," I blushed.

It was hard to believe the big changes in my parents. They didn't even seem like the same people. It wasn't anything physical. They looked exactly the same from the outside. It was their behavior and the way they talked that was different. They seemed less stressed, they smiled more, and overall, they both had positive attitudes. They just seemed happier.

After maybe an hour of being at the house and my dad still not making conversation, he tried to pull me aside to talk to me.

"Can I talk to you Roberto?" he whispers to me.

"Sure. What is it?"

"In private."

"Oh. Okay …" I looked over at Hunter, and he looked as if he understood my concern. I wasn't sure how to respond to the request.

But I didn't want to get Hunter worked up. I just smiled at him and said, "I'll be back in a second, Hunter." I looked at my mother and said, "Go easy on him."

I could tell that something was bothering my father. He seemed to be mad but was trying hard to contain his anger. He took me into the master bedroom and closed the door behind him. That scared me a little.

"What is he doing here?" he asked bluntly.

"Dad, I told you I was gay years ago."

"I know that! I'm not an idiot. I remember that conversation."

"Then, what's the problem?"

"What are you doing with someone who's an atheist?"

I couldn't help but laugh a bit and said, "Dad, he's not an atheist. He believes in a higher power. Yes, he believes that there is a God, but he isn't attached to any religion … at least not anymore. He was a practicing Mormon and had a terrible experience with his church. Too long to explain, but he's in a good place now."

"So he's spiritual, not religious?" he asked.

"Yes. Is that okay with you?"

He thought about it for a bit and said, "Well, as long as he believes in God, then I guess it's okay with me." What a relief! Those few brief words cut through the tension that had lingered since our arrival, and we both actually laughed. Then there was a long pause before he started again.

"Are you truly happy, kid?" he asked.

"The happiest I have ever been. He treats me well … better than well. He makes me feel like I can do anything in the world. I feel nothing but love and support. I see him, and I know that everything will be okay. I couldn't see myself without him."

"Well …okay then. I'm happy for you. All I want is for you is to be happy. I know I was a shitty father while you were growing up. I was stubborn, and refused to truly see what was important: the love and support of family. You made me think differently. After you left … it kind of shook me. Plus, your mother gave me a good earful."

He gave me a big hug, a real hug. The hug of a father who loves his son. I know he wasn't a perfect father, but really, who is perfect? I know we had a rough relationship in the beginning, but that was all in the past. Before me stood a different man: he was nicer, seemed happier and he smiled a lot more, even if he did still have a stubborn streak. His guard was finally down, and he wasn't afraid to show his feelings. I came back to the living room where Hunter and my mother were still chatting away.

Hunter looked over to me and asked, "Everything okay?"

"Perfect," I replied

"Okay, great!"

My brother Raul, sister Sofia, Aunt Mary, Uncle Eddie, their three girls and my grandparents all came by a few minutes later. My parents had made this visit into a big get-together party. They had the back yard barbecue grill flaming through a mound of charcoal. They set up a big plastic tent with tables and chairs. I was so happy to see everyone and to introduce Hunter to them.

My parents broiled Carne Asada, and made all kinds of salsa, accompanied by guacamole and homemade tortilla chips.

"Do you think it's time to tell them the big news?" Hunter hinted.

"Yeah. They are all here."

I stood up and quietly went over to the stereo to turn off the music that was playing. As soon as the music went away, I was met with boos and jeers from the crowd. I waved my hands up and down signaling for my raucous family to pipe down.

When they finally settled down I said, "Sorry to disturb the party, but I need all your attention. I just wanted to take this time to let you all know that Hunter and I are getting married." My family screamed and cheered. Every one of them hugged us.

Though busy at the grill keeping the food flowing and not burning, my dad flashed me a smile in support. Seeing that smile spread across his face meant the world to me. After so many problems in the past we were finally going to be a happy, united family.

Chapter Thirteen:

Final Bachelor Days

Three months away from the big wedding day, Hunter and I decided to hire some help with putting together the ceremony and the reception. We knew what we wanted in general but didn't exactly know how to execute it.

We got help from Francis Gutridge, a professional wedding planner who came highly recommended. Francis – who insisted on being called Fran – was an energetic, 5'8", young angelic blonde with highlighted tips and an overall flamboyant nature. I loved his silliness, but when it came to his work, Fran was quite sophisticated. When we told him about our simple but elegant black and white themed wedding, he had as many ideas as a peacock has colors.

When he spoke, I could tell he was very worldly, cultured, and adaptable to any situation. He absolutely lived for weddings.

I was thrilled to have his help, even if it cost an arm and a leg for his services. Hunter and I gave Francis our budget for a guest list of thirty, along with a few keywords as to what we wanted, and he was free to do as he wished. I wanted to be surprised. The few things we asked him to highlight in the wedding were recognition of a gay union, black and white for our colors, and a simple yet elegant presentation.

I told Hunter that I didn't want a big wedding. In fact, I had even suggested the idea of us going to City Hall, but he insisted that we do something special in front of my family.

"We are only getting married once, so lets celebrate it with as many people as we can," he said. The problem was that I felt weird having any kind of party or ceremony because of his family. Hunter hadn't spoken to his family since he had told them that he was gay. After that conversation, they basically banned him from their lives, and I was one hundred percent certain that they wouldn't attend our wedding. That's why I didn't want to make a big fuss about it.

Hunter sensed that was the reason I was holding back and said, "I know it would only be us two, close friends, and just your family. Please, don't be sad for me because my family won't be there … as long as I have you by my side, then that is all I'll need. You are all I'll ever need. I want an audience, so I can proudly tell the world that I love you and that I am yours."

"You sure?" I asked.

"Yes. It'll make me happy … the happiest man

alive."

"Okay. Whatever you want." I wanted to make him happy, so I, of course, went along with it.

The morning before the big day, Hunter and I arrived at the Santa Barbara Four Seasons Hotel, where the wedding and the celebration was going to happen in two different function rooms. Since we were spending a good amount of money to have it in the hotel and arranged rooms for everyone on our guest list who confirmed that they were coming, the hotel's manager of banquets gave us a good deal and even upgraded us to the executive premier room.

The accommodations were amazing, and once we were checked in, we stripped down to our underwear and cuddled one another to sleep. When I woke up a few hours later, Hunter had lunch all ready for us: turkey burgers, steak fries and soda, with a salad and dressing on the side. He knew me so well.

As we were eating, he said, "So I was thinking, since we are by ourselves all day today and everyone else arrives tomorrow morning …"

"Yeah … what do you have planned?" I asked curiously.

"I was thinking of having a combined but private bachelor party."

"Oh, you were, huh?"

"I figured, why not? It's our last night before we are a married couple. Let's do something crazy."

"What do you have in mind?"

"I'll take care of it. Just be ready in a few hours."

"Okay."

"By the way … how crazy do you want to go?"

"I'm open-minded. I'll go along with it. I'll leave it up to you."

"I'll think of something," he said.

Three hours went by and I was ready for this bachelor party. Hunter was ready, too, and he was sitting next to me on the couch when suddenly his phone rang.

"I'll be right out," he told the caller, and then hung up. "Time for some fun. I'll be right back," he told me, and out the door he went. Five minutes later, he returned with two super-handsome men: 6' 1" light-skinned black guy with a buzz cut, and an equally hot 6'2" Italian stud. They were both in their early 30s and wearing tuxedos. I shook their hands as they introduced themselves to me. Their names were Angelo and Marcus. They were sweet and had a heck of a handshake. They asked us to sit back and relax on the couch.

As the guys danced to the music, I kissed Hunter and he handed me a handful of dollar bills. We both had a dancer on us, stripping slowly and hovering over us with their sexy bodies. They were definitely built for this type of dancing – big and muscular. They were both wearing boxer-briefs which looked two sizes too small, and – oh, God – were they hung. Throughout, they would do a whiplash or swinging movement with their penises – it was an amazing sight. My dancer was so close that his penis kept slapping me on the chin. Hunter was getting similar treatment from his Italian dancer.

I started putting money in their underwear and in the guy's mouth…his idea, not mine. They gave a great lap dance and were eventually completely naked. Touching was allowed with them, since they were the ones leading our hands all over their bodies … and I mean all over.

Then, my guy said, "Time for the massage." Hunter and I got naked and laid face down on the bed side by side. The guys did their nude massages on top of us, and they were actually pretty amazing at it.

Hunter turns to me and asked, "Are you enjoying yourself?"

"I am."

"Good. You did say crazy."

"You delivered!" Marcus and Angelo then told us that for a little more money, we could have sex with them.

I looked at Hunter and said, "Not today but thank you."

"Yeah," Hunter agreed, "but we appreciate the offer." They seemed genuinely disappointed.

After the strippers left, Hunter and I were so worked up that we had our own sexy time, which lasted a good hour-and-a-half. He kissed me and fell asleep right after we were done. I, on the other hand, had so much on my mind that I couldn't fall asleep. I grabbed my bathrobe, tipped-toed away from the bed, and headed toward the balcony. I sat on the chair looking out at the stars and moon. I kept thinking about all of my family and friends that were coming into town to see us get married. I had hoped that everyone made it okay and that they were all comfortable. I wondered how everything would look and questioned the wisdom of us trusting Francis with the massive amount of detailed work and planning for this wedding. Could one man handle it alone?

My mind shot straight into panic mode. I started second-guessing everything. Was I getting cold feet? Was this what I really wanted? Was this a realistic dream? Was Hunter the right man for me?

I only wanted to get married once, and I never wanted to go through a divorce. I needed to be sure. Then, I remembered that scared little kid I was … hiding, hating myself and who I was as a person, attempting suicide … and I remembered how far I had come.

I walked back into the room. I looked at Hunter sleeping so peacefully … angelic and perfect. All of my insecurities evaporated in an instant. Of course I wanted to marry him. I wanted him to be right next to me for the rest of my life's journey.

I look at him and he makes me feel whole. He makes me happy. I trust my heart, and he's the one for me. He's always been.

This reminded me that I needed to work on my vows. After I was done, I thought I might have overdone it and made them a little too long, but I was sticking with them. I slipped into the bed and snuggled myself to sleep.

Chapter Fourteen:

Tying The Knot

Fran took Hunter and me into the reception space early on the morning of our wedding day, still comfortable in our pajamas. As we entered the room, I could not believe what I saw. Boy, did he deliver!

Tears ran down my face. Emotions I can't describe shot through my body. He created an artistic vision I'd never in a million years conceive of on my own. The whole thing seemed surreal in its elegance and beauty. This was exactly what I wanted without really knowing that I wanted it.

He walked us through the entire decoration scheme and his ingenious wedding plans. The reception hall was filled with lots of light, with white and black everywhere, but not to the point where it looked busy or tacky. Everything looked very expensive. All of the centerpieces were filled with white lilies and some black flower with a touch of green. He used mood lighting to create luxurious effects and highlighted focus areas. He told us that he had trouble finding a way to incorporate the gay part of the wedding besides the two of us getting married. He said that he went ahead and called in a favor from one of his friends.

A well-known and extremely beautiful drag queen would officiate the ceremony … she was licensed and ready to lead us in taking our vows. To me, that was really exciting and a nice touch! Our wedding cake had two white dove cake toppers wearing black bow ties. They were kissing each other, and the cake was entirely covered in white fondant, four layers high, with what looked like crystals all around, and a hint of black lines around the bottom of every layer. It was exactly what Hunter and I wanted. Now, I couldn't wait to get married.

Walking into the Mariposa Garden, Hunter and I stood in front of a two-pole canopy facing a spectacular view of the Pacific Ocean and the Channel Islands. It was decorated with vines and white lisianthus flowers. We both wore matching and fitted light-brown, two-button, blue-and-gold plaid deco suits and dark blue ties that had white polka-dots. The garden was flanked by beautiful Spanish adobe architecture and red tile roofs. On the grass were rows of Chiavari chairs draped in white fabric tied with nosegay flowers, and hanging bouquet arrangements were set down the aisle.

Standing in between Hunter and me was Miss Alada Mann, the fabulous and well-known drag queen superstar who was officiating the wedding. She was a fierce queen that could easily be mistaken for Beyonce's twin. She was wearing a big, curly Diana Ross wig, and like a gilded goddess, she wore a one-shoulder, metallic gown that hit the floor. She gave us a hug and kissed both cheeks.

"You sexy beasts ready?" she asked.

"Yes," we said in unison.

"Great. Thank you for having me. You two are my first."

Wedding guests slowly streamed inside. As expected, not a single member of Hunter's family showed up. My family and friends did something I wasn't expecting, but from what I hear they gave Francis Gutridge the idea. The room was being divided between genders as they walked in. All of the women were seated on the left side and all of the men were on the right side. Hunter began to cry a little: this really touched him.

Everyone we loved was there to support our union. On the women's side was my mother, my sister Sofia, Dawn

(Hunter's "fruit fly"), my grandma Estela, my aunt Mary and her three daughters, my hag Rose and my lesbian friend Amber, accompanied by her girlfriend. On the men's side was my father, my brother Raul, my best buddy Sheldon, my grandpa Joshua, my uncle Eddie, my landlord Ralph, my agent Mark, Jan the Czech, Ben the Puerto Rican and even my good buddy Marco Ellis Ward. The rest of the guests were model friends of mine and some of Hunter's lawyer friends from his firm, which made a total guest list of 30.

The wedding march song began, but it had a fast beat to it. It was loud but got everyone smiling and dancing, especially when Miss Alada Mann began to sing along with the music. She could easily be a winning contestant on The Voice or another competitive singing show. She made the whole service feel so wonderful. She was funny, honest, and serious when she needed to be.

She read this beautiful poem about love. Maybe what I appreciated most is that she personally thanked my family for being there, choosing to be an integral part of their son's joyous day. She made everyone feel included.

As if announcing the arrival of royalty, she declared, "It's time for the vows. The couple has prepared their own. Roberto, please go first."

I cleared my throat. Nervous? That's an understatement! I didn't think I would get the words out, but somehow I managed: "Ever since I was little, I didn't think I would ever be up here exchanging rings with the one I love, because I thought that was only a 'straight people thing.' I'm happy I was wrong, and glad I could share this moment today with you and the people that I love."

"You make me feel whole. I may not be the smartest man in the world, but the one thing I do know is that you and I are meant to be together. You are my hero, my one true love, and my inspiration. You make me want to be a better man."

"I love you unconditionally and without hesitation. I vow to love you, encourage you, trust you and respect you. As a family, we will create a home filled with learning, laughter and compassion. I promise to work with you to foster and cherish a relationship of equality, knowing that together we will build a life far better than either of us could imagine alone. Today, I choose you to be my husband. I accept you as you are, and I offer myself in return: I will care for you, stand beside you, and share with you all of life's adversities and all of its joys from this day forward, and all the days of my life."

The whole room was in tears including my soon-to-be husband.

Miss Alada Mann said, " That was beautiful honey, but please don't make me cry again, because fixing this make up is a bitch!" Boy could she work a room! She was hilarious.

Then she said, "Sure you don't want to marry me instead? I'm kidding! Kind of ..." The whole room laughed again. She had a way of keeping things fun and light. She was a natural performer.

"Okay, Hunter now it's your turn. Whenever you are ready," said Miss Alada Mann.

Hunter wiped away his tears and cleared his throat. "How do you top that?" Everyone laughed. "I completely forgot what I was going to say, but Miss Alada, he's mine!" They laughed even harder. I was surprised at his great comedic timing.

He waited until they stopped laughing, and began to speak again. "I'm honored to take you, Roberto, as my husband, my best friend, the love of my life, and my soul mate forever. The love you give to me is more than any person can ever hope for, and I'm thankful for that every single day."

"So, in the presence of God, family, and our friends, I offer you my solemn vow to be with you always; in sickness and in health; in good times and bad; in times of joy as well as in sorrow. I promise to love you unconditionally, to support all of your goals, to honor and respect you, to laugh and cry with you and to make strawberry-and-Nutella crepes whenever you want them. So with these rings that we will be exchanging in a few minutes, I give you my hand. I've given you my heart and my love for as long as both we shall live."

Miss Alada Mann broke the silence, "That was beautiful, and I love Nutella." Again she had the audience in stitches. "Can we get the rings out?" she bellowed in a purposely loud voice.

We took out the rings from their little boxes.

Miss Alada Mann continued, "As we look at these rings, they are symbols of love: circular in shape, knowing that love is also infinite and never ending. Today, as you exchange these rings, you will always have these symbols of each other as life partners and as friends. Roberto, can you get the first ring and place it on Hunter's finger, and repeat after me?"

"Okay," I said softly as I held Hunter's hand and wiggled the gold ring onto his finger.

As Miss Alada Mann directed, I repeated everything she said: "With this ring. I thee wed. And with it, I give my love to you, and only you, as long as we both shall live.

"Now … your turn, Hunter," she said, as Hunter also repeated everything she said. "With this ring. I thee wed. And with it, I give my love to you, and only you, as long as we both shall live.

Hunter had a hard time slipping my finger into the gold band, and when it finally was on he said, "Well, at least I know it'll never come off." That probably made the audience laugh the most during the ceremony.

"Now, I would like both of you to turn to your audience," she said. We did. "We know that love and marriage are not always easy. When times get difficult, remember these are the people who have come here to support you today, and who will be there to support you throughout the time that you are together. If you ever need to call someone …" She paused

and addressed the guests: "Don't send them to voicemail …
ya'll pick up!"

Besides being beautiful, our ceremony was the most
wickedly hilarious I could imagine. The audience wasn't bored
and solemn. Unlike at a formal church ceremony where
everyone sits like statues, bored and stiff, they were totally
immersed in the moment and thrilled to be there.

This was what a marriage ceremony should be. Not an
overly-somber show to impress others, but a special moment
that friends and family would remember with fondness.

Miss Alada Mann kept the ceremony rolling. "I can see
that they love you. So can you just say 'I do' after you pledge
to be friends, a family, neighbors, and to love these two as
much as they love each other?"

The guest party said, "I do," in unison.

In that brief second when all the guests said, "I do," my
mind briefly zoned out. My eyes were scanning the crowd and
simultaneously I saw dozens of lips say those two magical
words giving their unconditional love and support. I was not

fast enough to see my father in that precise moment, but I will believe to my dying day he said it, and meant it, along with the rest.

Miss Alada Mann was still entertaining the crowd but my mind was filled with so many thoughts I didn't hear a word. All I could think about was all the times I'd been with someone who didn't share my vision for the future. Now, I have Hunter. And Hunter has me… for better or for worse. I'm not perfect, but Hunter brings out the best in me.

This life -- out and strong -- has just begun, and I can't wait to see what is ahead for us! I have Hunter's unconditional support and—

"Roberto!" shouted Miss Alada Mann, for what I'm guessing was at least the second time. My face turned red in embarrassment. I really had zoned out completely.

"Back with the living, hon? Dreaming about that honeymoon?"

If there was a high point of gaiety in the ceremony, that was it. People laughed so much they had to wipe tears from their eyes.

"Alright!" Miss Alada Mann exclaimed. Her antics hit their funny bone again, but she pressed on despite the laughter. "Now, this is my favorite part. So now, by the power vested in me by the American marriage industry and the state of California and 45 minutes on the internet …"

Miss Alada Mann: comic genius.

She finished, " I now pronounce you husband and husband! You may now kiss each other."

As I leaned in to kiss Hunter, I'd like to brag about thinking of something poetic and profound. But that would be a lie. Amidst the cheering my mind was as blank as my emotions were ablaze. I loved Hunter so much and what I experienced in that glorious kiss is beyond words.

About the Author: Marcelino Rosas is a California native who was raised in the heart of Los Angeles. He lives, writes, and was educated in Los Angeles. He comes from an active family who enjoys playing all kinds of sports. He's a movie collector, writer, editor, and now author. Marcelino studied kinesiology to become a teacher and coach but is now mostly known for his modeling work. Ever since he won an essay writing contest for Disney in the third grade, he gained a passion for writing and telling stories. He felt he had a powerful, moving story to tell, so he decided to write. He hopes that his two novels '*Afuera*: A Young Latino's Journey' and '*Fuerte*: A Journey Continued' will inspire teens and young adults struggling with the same issues that the main character did. Hopefully it has the power and the potential to touch many

 lives.

Write up by:

Phillip J. Bartell

www.ingramcontent.com/pod-product-compliance
Lightning Source LLC
Chambersburg PA
CBHW060943180626
46817CB00004B/1690